"Lori…"

He stood but when he walked toward her, she stepped behind a chair, effectively placing a barrier between them. "I didn't want to lie to you. You have to believe me."

"It doesn't matter, Troy—*Trey*…" She crossed her arms beneath her midriff, her gaze holding his. "It's good we both learned the truth now before either one of us became emotionally attached to the other. This way, nobody gets hurt."

Was she kidding? He stared at her but she didn't blink or look away. At last he shrugged. "Yeah, right." He pulled the door open, pausing once more to look back at her. "I'll send you my address."

She didn't move or reply. He left, feeling as if he'd been punched in the gut, re̶ burning a hole in his heart.

Dear Reader,

I've always been fascinated by stories involving a miscarriage of justice—*and* exploring that issue in THE McCLOUDS series has been a challenge I've enjoyed. Many people hold a deep and compelling belief that justice should prevail—the "good guys" should win and the "bad guys" should fall. In a perfect world perhaps that might happen, but in the real world perfection is difficult to achieve.

Trey Harper was only twelve years old when he vowed to right the wrong caused by Lonnie Kerrigan. He believes Lonnie is responsible for his brother's death, and he's determined justice will win out and Lonnie will pay. As an adult, Trey remains committed to his quest for justice and to exonerating Chase McCloud. I hope you enjoy Trey and Lori's story, as well as Luke, Jessie and Chase's, as much as I've enjoyed writing them.

Warmest wishes,

Lois Faye Dyer

www.LoisDyer.com

TREY'S SECRET

LOIS FAYE DYER

SPECIAL EDITION

Published by Silhouette Books

America's Publisher of Contemporary Romance

SILHOUETTE BOOKS

ISBN-13: 978-0-373-24823-0
ISBN-10:   0-373-24823-7

TREY'S SECRET

Visit Silhouette Books at www.eHarlequin.com

Printed in U.S.A.

Books by Lois Faye Dyer

Silhouette Special Edition

Lonesome Cowboy #1038
He's Got His Daddy's Eyes #1129
The Cowboy Takes a Wife #1198
The Only Cowboy for Caitlin #1253
Cattleman's Courtship #1306
Cattleman's Bride-to-Be #1457
Practice Makes Pregnant #1569
Cattleman's Heart #1611
The Prince's Bride #1640
Luke's Proposal #1745
Jesse's Child #1776
Chase's Promise #1791
Trey's Secret #1823

* The McClouds of Montana

LOIS FAYE DYER

lives on Washington State's beautiful Puget Sound with her husband, their yellow Lab, Maggie Mae, and two eccentric cats. She loves to hear from readers and you can write to her c/o Paperbacks Plus, 1618 Bay Street, Port Orchard, WA 98366.

In memory of my uncle, Karl Jacobson,
of Akra, Norway. The world is lesser
for his absence.

Chapter One

Wolf Creek, Montana
Early Spring

On a windswept hilltop a mile outside Wolf Creek, twelve-year-old Trey Harper hunched his shoulders against the spatter of raindrops that chilled his face and hands. Beside him, his twin sister Raine shivered and tucked her chin lower into the neckline of her hooded sweatshirt.

They lay flat on their bellies, hiding behind a three-foot-tall sagebrush. Scattered chunks of shale littered the hard clay and sand soil beneath them. When Trey leaned to his left and peered around the lowest branches of the bush, he had a clear view of the cemetery below. A single, uniformed officer stood several feet behind the grieving family while the other black-clad mourners clustered across the open grave.

"He looks different," Raine said, her voice troubled. "Don't you think Chase looks different, Trey?"

He stared intently at the group of McClouds. "He looks sad." *Of course he does. His grandpa Angus is in that coffin.* Trey knew about being sad at funerals. Their older brother, Mike, had been buried barely three months ago. "And older. Maybe thinner. I wonder if he gets good food in jail?" *And I wonder if he minds having that cop standing behind him, watching him.*

"I hope so."

Below them the pastor lifted his Bible and began to read. The faint sound of his voice reached them, although Trey couldn't make out the words.

"I miss Mike," Raine continued, her voice breaking. "And I miss Chase, too. I wish this year had never happened."

Trey hoped she didn't start crying again but he

thought she might. He always knew when Raine was upset, just as she seemed to know the same about him. Their mother said twins were telepathic. He didn't know why his mom seemed to think it was such a big deal. They were brother and sister, that's all.

"Well, it did." He couldn't look at her, afraid that if he saw tears on her face, he'd cry, too. Guys his age didn't do that.

"I don't believe Chase hurt Mike on purpose, do you?"

"People say he did. Mom believes he did." Trey didn't like to think about his mom. She'd started staying in bed after Mike's funeral. He rarely saw her dressed in anything except her nightgown and robe anymore. Sometimes he was afraid she'd never come out of her bedroom again. And the sound of her soft weeping behind the closed door made his heart hurt.

Even his dad had stopped smiling and, despite his and Raine's efforts to get him to eat the dinners they made after school, he was losing weight. His jeans hung loose on his hips and the bones of his face seemed to stick out more each day. And too often Trey could smell the sweet odor of whiskey when his Dad got home from work.

Maybe if Raine and I were better cooks, Dad and Mom would eat more, he thought gloomily. *I'm really tired of mac and cheese and hamburgers, too.*

"Dad said Chase says he didn't." Raine's comment broke into Trey's thoughts. "Do you think he did?"

"No." Trey looked at her. Her gray eyes were anxious. "I don't."

"Me, neither." Her gaze left his to focus on the group in the cemetery below. "But he's still gone away and we never get to see him—just like Mike. Only Mike's dead and Chase isn't. Do you think Chase will ever come back?"

"I don't know." *I want him to,* he thought fiercely. *I know Mike never can, but Chase could. He's like my other brother and he can help me make Lonnie Kerrigan pay for what he did to Mike.* Maybe life would be normal again if Chase came home. He wasn't sure how he could change things, though, unless he could find a way to prove Chase hadn't been driving his truck when it crashed into Mike's car. But that seemed impossible. "Maybe someday, when I find out what really happened."

"Do you think Mom will believe you?"

"Probably not." His voice was bleak as the swift

mental image popped into his head of his mother as he'd last seen her, drifting around the darkened house like a ghost. *But I'll find out, anyway. Chase wouldn't lie, and he said it was Lonnie's fault Mike wrecked his car.* Losing their brother, Mike, had been devastating, but losing Chase, too, had made Mike's death that much worse. The two older boys had spent long hours hanging out at the Harper family home. Chase was cool. He'd let Trey tag along with them, even if Mike hadn't wanted him to. Now they both were gone, and he felt as if a giant hole had been blown in his world.

Down in the cemetery, the small crowd of mourners stirred, some paying their respects to the McCloud family while others moved toward the parked cars.

"Come on, Raine." Trey used his elbows and the toes of his sneakers to maneuver backward. "We don't want anyone to see us. We'll be in trouble with Dad for sure if he knows we came out here."

Rocks and twigs scratched his palms. When the slope of the hill hid them from view, he stood, and with Raine close on his heels, they raced to their bikes. Soon they were pedaling furiously down the little-used dirt road back to town, intent on reaching home before they were missed.

Fifteen years later
Wolf Creek, Montana

"Raine, you're too sick to leave the house." Trey frowned at his sister. The afternoon sunlight slanted through the window, highlighting the slender form on the blue sofa. Her legs were tucked beneath her and her head rested against the cushion. Her face was flushed and her gray eyes seemed bright with fever.

"I have a summer cold," she insisted. "That's all." She stopped talking as a sudden bout of coughing doubled her over.

Trey handed her a glass of water and a box of Kleenex from the coffee table. "It may be a cold but I bet you've got a fever." He laid his palm against her cheek.

Raine ducked away from him before he could do more than register the heat radiating from her skin. She glared at him and sneezed. "Sometimes I run a temperature when I have a cold." She dabbed at her watering eyes with a tissue. "It's no big deal. I'll be fine by tonight."

He sighed. "Be reasonable, Raine. Chances are this trip is a dead end and the letter just an attempt to con us into handing over money. The writer didn't say there was any hard evidence."

"Nevertheless—" Raine's chin jutted with determination "—it's the first new clue in fifteen years. Don't try to convince me you aren't dying to find out who wrote it, Trey, because I know you are."

"I'm interested," he acknowledged. "But that doesn't mean I think we'll find out at the Bull 'n' Bash who caused the crash that killed Mike." He glanced at the framed photo hanging on the wall behind Raine, taken at their ninth birthday. Their mother smiled sunnily at the camera, her arm around their father's waist. Standing beside her was a laughing fourteen-year-old Mike, and in front were Trey and Raine. The happy faces in the photo conveyed no inkling that a short three years later, Mike would die in an automobile accident and life as Trey knew it would change forever. Within six years, both his parents were dead, too. Though the official medical ruling for his mother's passing was a heart attack and, in the case of his dad, swift-moving lung cancer, he'd always believed their deaths were accelerated by their broken hearts. They'd kept going through the motions of living after they lost their oldest son, but some essential part of his parents had died with Mike. Now he and his sister were the only remaining members of a once-happy family.

"At least there's a chance. Maybe it's a slim one, but it's more than we've had before," Raine said, interrupting his thoughts.

"Still not a good enough reason for you to leave the house when you're ill. Besides," Trey added, "the Bull 'n' Bash is a rough place. I'd feel better if you weren't with me."

"I've been in dodgy bars before," Raine told him, her expression stubborn.

Trey glanced at his watch. "It's four hours before I leave for Billings. Get some sleep. If you're feeling better later, we'll talk about this then."

"Fine." Raine sneezed and shuffled off to her bedroom.

Trey shook his head and let himself out of her house, closing the door quietly behind him. He didn't think she was well enough to make the three-hour trip to Billings, let alone spend the evening in a crowded bar, followed by another long drive back home. Besides, the person he was meeting might not have information about their older brother's death.

The desire to learn what really happened to Mike that terrible night still burned as hot and strong in Trey as it had all those years ago. If anything, his curiosity to know the truth had grown more intense with time. He had to check out the letter—he couldn't ignore it. Neither he nor Raine believed Chase McCloud had been responsible for the highway smash that ended Mike's life. The attorneys hired by Chase's family had done their best, but he'd been convicted of vehicular manslaughter and, at seventeen, incarcerated in a Montana state juvenile facility for three years.

Trey had seen him only once in the decade and a half since he and Raine had hidden on the hill and watched the burial of Angus McCloud. During his senior year in high school, he'd heard a rumor Chase was visiting his parents. He'd driven out to the McCloud property and found him alone in the horse barn. But this wasn't the laughing teenager he remembered, this was an older, harder man. When he'd told Chase he wanted to help him find evidence that would prove to the world he hadn't killed Mike, Chase had stared at him, his eyes cold as winter.

He'd never forgotten Chase's words. *Mike's death is old history, kid. Forget it and get on with your life. You can't live in the past and you can't change it.*

He'd tried taking Chase's advice. But fifteen years after the accident, Trey still wanted to explore any lead that might prove his theory that Lonnie Kerrigan should have been convicted of causing Mike's death, not Chase, the man who had loved his friend like a brother.

The injustice nagged at him like a sore tooth.

The wall thermometer mounted on the corner post of Raine's porch read ninety-four degrees. Heat shimmered in waves above the concrete sidewalk, the air heavy with the rich fragrance of the roses edging the path. He settled his Stetson lower over his brow, shielding his eyes from the late-afternoon sun that slanted low over the small ranching community of Wolf Creek. Tall old maple trees lined the broad avenues in Raine's neighborhood of family bungalows, located only ten blocks from Main Street. Within minutes Trey was locking his car in the alley that ran behind the Wolf Creek Saloon and Restaurant, grateful as always that he and Raine, both business owners, had assigned parking slots.

His apartment above the saloon was cool and dim, the air conditioner humming softly to keep the sweltering heat outside at bay and the interior at a comfortable seventy degrees.

He dropped his hat and keys on the kitchen counter, checked his machine for phone messages and left almost immediately to jog down the stairs and into the bar through the alley door.

"How's Raine feeling?" The bartender wore jeans

and a pristine white T-shirt with Wolf Creek Saloon printed across the front, his silver hair military short.

"Not good, Sam." Trey joined him behind the long, circa-1880's polished bar. He dropped ice in a tall glass and filled it with water, which he drained in three swallows, then held it under the spigot again. "I'm sure she has a fever, but she won't admit it's anything except a simple cold."

"Huh," Sam grunted. "I suppose she's insisting she'll be at work tomorrow?"

"Yeah." Trey shook his head. "She's got to be the most stubborn woman on earth."

"She's got a mind of her own," Sam agreed. "Always has."

Trey leaned his elbows on the gleaming surface of the mahogany counter and swept the room with an assessing gaze. Barely a third of the tables and booths were full and only a quarter of the comfortable bar stools held customers. He knew the relative quiet would quickly disappear when the evening crowd arrived, especially as one of the regular evening-shift waitresses had called in sick. Trey wondered briefly if she was suffering from the same symptoms as Raine. "You think you'll be okay here tonight with only Sheila and Rocky to help?"

"We can manage." Sam winked. "If the crowd

gets too rowdy, I'll hit the panic button and the Sheriff's Office will send a deputy over to break it up. Don't worry about us."

The possibility of Sam calling the sheriff to break up a fight was so unlikely that Trey had to laugh. "Nevertheless, I hate to leave you short-staffed. If I could, I'd reschedule my meeting."

Sam snorted. "Your dad and me ran this place when you and Raine were still in diapers. I think I can manage to keep things ticking over for one night without your help."

"Hell, Sam," Trey said with amused affection. "You could probably run this place single-handed. What was I thinking?"

"Damned if I know," the older man grunted in mild affront, but his eyes twinkled. "Once you're sixty years old, like me, you'll stop worrying about all this minor stuff."

Trey stayed in the saloon for a while, chatting with Sam and the occasional customer, then he left to check in with the restaurant staff and found the busy kitchen functioning smoothly under the guidance of Raine's assistant, Charlotte. He strolled through the dining room, pausing to say hello to many of the familiar diners, before heading back upstairs to shower and change.

Hoping to fade into the crowd at the Bull 'n' Bash, he purposely chose to wear a plain black Western shirt with pearl snaps, faded Levis, and his favorite black cowboy boots.

Deciding not to call Raine, within the hour he was driving south from Wolf Creek toward Billings.

Eleven hours later

He was lying face-down in a roadside ditch. The half inch of water covering the dirt and gravel beneath him had soaked the front of his shirt and jeans. The tarry smell of hot asphalt, the scent of sun-dried weeds and the sharp bite of sagebrush mixed with the smell of damp earth.

He stirred, grimacing when his cheek scraped over something hard, cold and wet. Opening his eyes required concentrated effort, and when he lifted his head, pain shafted through his right temple. He squinted, clenching his teeth against the agony, and looked about him.

He pushed to his hands and knees, swaying as he fought off a wave of dizziness before he stood. Staggering sideways, he struggled to stay upright.

The hurt in his head was vicious, pounding in time with the beat of his pulse. He brushed his fingers over his forehead, then held his hand inches from his half-closed eyes. Rust-colored blood mingled with traces of bright scarlet on his fingertips.

"Damn." The smears were visible proof that the pain wasn't just from a bad headache. The sore, bruised muscles in the rest of his body made him wonder how long he'd been lying unconscious in the ditch.

Where the hell am I?

Shielding his eyes with his hand, against the sun's rays, he turned carefully, looking up and down the stretch of blacktop. Acres of rolling prairie edged the road on both sides and were lined with barbed-wire fences, but he could see no cattle or horses, not even wild deer or antelope.

In fact, he realized, he was alone except for a hawk soaring high above him in the cloudless sky. The sun was low on the horizon but its rays were already hot on his face and hands. Given the clear quality of the light and the dew still beading the coarse roadside grass, he thought it must be early morning, maybe 7:00 or 8:00 a.m.

He glanced at his wrist to confirm his guess, but instead of his watch he saw only a lighter band of skin against the darker tan of his arm. Frowning, he shoved his hands into his front jeans pockets. They were empty, as were the back ones. The long-sleeved cotton shirt he wore had a breast pocket, but a quick check netted only an empty gum wrapper.

"Son of a bitch!" he muttered out loud.

Without thinking, he bent over, wincing at the instant throbbing in his head, and checked the inside of his left cowboy boot. A pocket in the lining held a folded hundred-dollar bill, and an identical compartment in the right one contained a knife. He hefted the balanced weight of the blade, relieved to find something familiar.

He had the feeling there should have been something else in his pockets but trying to remember what was missing sent shards of pain shafting through his temple. Carefully keeping his head as still as possible, he turned his body until he could see the length of the ditch where he'd been lying. An envelope lay half-hidden in a tuft of flattened rough grass.

The gravel lining the shallow ditch rolled beneath his feet as he half walked, half slid to reach the bottom and bent to retrieve the paper.

The envelope was wet and dripped water onto his boots when he picked it up. All that remained of the address were a few damp streaks of smeared blue ink. Only the postmark was legible, half-covering the stamp in the top right corner.

"Granger, Montana," he read aloud. The place didn't seem familiar.

He slid a single sheet of folded paper from the envelope. The note was typewritten, and the ink unsmudged. "If you want to know what really happened the night your brother died, come to the Bull 'n' Bash this Friday at midnight."

The cryptic sentence did nothing to clear up his confusion.

Did the letter belong to him? Or was it merely trash, tossed into the ditch from some passing vehicle?

Again he stared at the postmark. Granger, Montana. It still didn't ring any bells. He didn't live there. He lived in…

He went totally still, bracing against a wave of shock. He not only didn't know where he lived, he didn't know who he was.

Stunned, he searched his memory. He knew the jeans he wore were Levis but he couldn't recall his own name, nor where he came from, nor how he'd arrived on this deserted stretch of highway.

Distracted, he brushed absentmindedly at a

trickle of moisture on his cheek. His fingers came away wet with blood.

His attention caught by the crimson stain, he narrowed his eyes, considering what he did know.

First, he was bleeding from a cut on his head. Gingerly, he explored his temple and found a lump.

Correction, I'm bleeding from a cut probably caused by a blow from whatever blunt instrument gave me this bump.

Second, he couldn't remember a damn thing about himself. His pockets were empty—no wallet, no ID, no money except for the hundred-dollar bill hidden in his boot.

It made sense to assume he'd been robbed, he thought. But why would a thief have dumped him out along the road in the middle of nowhere?

Unless he knew the person who'd fleeced him? Maybe he'd been attacked in his car?

A swift, vivid image of a silver vehicle, a mud-spattered truck and two men, one of whom lifted a tire iron and swung it at him, flashed before his eyes. His stomach rolled as the memory washed through him and he relived the pain that followed the slam of the tire iron against his head and the sickening fall into oblivion when he lost consciousness.

Someone tried to kill me. The deep conviction

set off warning bells and keyed an adrenaline rush that kicked in his survival instinct. Ignoring the pounding agony in his head, he scanned the surrounding area once more, relieved when he found nothing threatening.

The low roar of an engine broke the quiet and a semi truck appeared around the curve in the highway some distance away. Exhaust billowed from tall silver pipes on each side of the cab, creating streaks of white against the deep blue sky and gray-green pastures.

What are the odds this might be someone coming back to make sure I'm dead?

On the other hand, if it wasn't, the big semi might be his chance to put miles between him and the lonely spot where they'd dumped his body. It was a gamble, but the brief flashback had revealed a silver SUV and a pickup truck, not a lumbering commercial semi.

He tucked the envelope and knife back into his boot, shoved the hundred-dollar bill into his jeans pocket and walked gingerly to the pavement's white center line.

I hope to hell the driver sees me in time. And that he isn't the guy that put me in the ditch.

The truck slowed as it neared, three blasts of the horn blaring a loud warning.

He lifted his arms and waved his hands over his head in an attempt to flag down the truck. Luckily, the big semi rumbled to a stop beside him, air brakes wheezing.

"What the hell happened to you?" The driver asked, peering down at him from the open window of the high cab.

"I've been robbed," he answered, thinking quickly. "Emptied my pockets and stole my car." He touched his temple, the brief pressure making it throb. "Left me a souvenir, too. Can you give me a lift to the nearest town?"

"Sure, climb in." The beefy driver jerked his head toward the passenger side.

Square black lettering spelled out Edward Brothers Cattle Company on the white painted door. He pulled it open and climbed up.

"Here." The driver handed him a stained but clean mechanics' towel when he'd settled into the seat and slammed the door. "You're bleeding."

"Thanks." He pressed the cloth to his temple.

"Bud Ames." The driver held out his hand.

"Ed Smith," he replied, inspired by the sign on the truck door. He knew it probably wasn't his real name, but it was easy enough to remember and for now, it would do.

"There's some ice in the cooler behind the seat," the driver said as he released the brake and shifted into gear. "Might help that knot you've got on your head. Where you bound?"

He hadn't a clue. Only one destination came to mind. "Granger," he replied.

The driver nodded. "I'm going through there. You can ride all the way with me or you can get out at the next town and have that cut looked at. There's a big truck stop on the outskirts so it should be easy to catch another ride if you decide to see a doc before heading for Granger."

"I think I'll get stitched up first."

"Your choice."

An hour later they turned off the highway and entered a small town.

"Where do you want me to drop you off?" The driver pointed out the windshield. "There's a clinic over yonder if you want to have your head seen to first, or the police station is a few blocks further on if you'd rather report bein' attacked."

He didn't need to weigh his options. The wound on his temple was raw and a headache pulsed behind his eyes. "The clinic."

The truck rumbled through the center of town, the storefronts growing fewer and interspersed with private homes before the trucker braked and pulled to the curb. "This is the clinic." He nodded at the single-story building just beyond the passenger's window. "You take care now. Good luck."

"Thanks for the ride." He held out his hand.

"No problem."

The semi with its load of cattle moved slowly off down the street as he entered the building.

Two hours later he left the emergency room with ten stitches in his head and his pocket lighter by eighty dollars. The nurse had shown him to a restroom where he'd washed the blood from his hands and face and brushed most of the dirt from his shirt and jeans. Luckily, the ditch had been lined with gravel, which kept the mud on his clothes to a minimum. Time and heat had dried his jeans and shirt. There was nothing he could do about the dark shadow of his beard—the restroom hadn't supplied a razor.

The doctor couldn't give him a definite time-table regarding the return of his memory. However, the MD had assured him that in his experience, cases of amnesia like his were often short-term and it was likely he'd start remembering things gradually over the next few weeks. While there was no magic pill that could restore his memory immediately, he was relieved to learn the loss probably wouldn't be permanent.

After declining the doctor's offer to refer him to the local social services agency for assistance, he left the clinic and paused on the sidewalk. Should he visit the local police and report the robbery?

He wasn't sure he should. While visiting the Sheriff's Office was his best chance of finding whether someone, somewhere, had reported him missing, he'd have to tell the sheriff he had amnesia. Which would surely set off a search for his next of kin, that couldn't be kept private and in the end might prove dangerous. If the sheriff's investigation alerted his attackers before his memory returned, how would he recognize the enemy? He might end up in a ditch again. Only next time he'd be dead.

Deciding to postpone a visit to the Sheriffs Office until he'd considered the situation from all possible angles, he headed back toward the highway. He'd grab a sandwich at the truck stop café and look for a driver willing to give him a ride to Granger.

Chapter Two

Lori Ashworth leaned against the kitchen counter, staring out the window into the backyard as she waited for the coffee to finish brewing. She cherished this part of the day when the house was quiet and she had an hour to herself before leaving for work at the Granger Bar and Restaurant.

On the countertop beside her, the coffeemaker gave a final gurgle and the light on the machine switched off. She carried her mug and a bowl of cereal outside to the patio table for her last chance to enjoy some solitude until the following morn-

ing. At 7:00 a.m., the sun's rays were already hot
on her bare arms and legs but lacked the burn they
would hold later. The lattice above her filtered the
sunlight over hanging cedar baskets filled with
begonias, geraniums and fuchsias that trailed
lush greenery and colorful blossoms toward the
concrete pad below.

For the past three months, these peaceful
breaks had gradually turned introspective. Ever
since she celebrated her twenty-fifth birthday,
she'd felt restless.

What's wrong with me?

She paused, spoon in hand and stared unseeingly at the expanse of emerald-green lawn. What
was it that stirred this vaguely unsettled feeling?

She pondered the question, thinking about her
life, and finally decided that perhaps it was
because she was stuck in neutral, romantically
speaking. She didn't feel lonely, exactly, and she
was far too busy to be bored. But she'd grown up
in Granger, and except for the four years she'd
spent in Missoula at college, she'd seen the same
people every week of her life. No thrills, no
intrigue—no guy making her heart beat faster.

Not that she was looking for a serious relationship, she thought, sipping her coffee. And she de-

finitely wasn't in the market for a husband since she barely had time to cope with her mother, the business and keeping her two younger siblings in college funds.

Still, she thought wistfully, it would be nice to have some excitement in my life. What woman wouldn't like a little romance?

The alarm on her watch went off, pulling her thoughts away from daydreaming and wishes. Ten minutes later she left the house for the six-block walk to the restaurant.

Just before 10:00 a.m., the moving van he'd hitched a ride with rolled into Granger, a medium-size ranching community with established neighborhoods and a few new houses on the outskirts. The main street was wide and uncrowded, lined on both sides with a variety of businesses. Though not a large town, it appeared prosperous.

He scanned the storefronts, wanting to feel a connection, to see a sign he knew or a face he recognized, anything that would tell him he belonged in Granger. Despite his hopes, he didn't have a gut-deep feeling telling him this was home.

He asked the driver to drop him at a stoplight, returning the man's wave as he climbed down from the cab. The big truck lumbered away down the road and he set off along the sidewalk. Halfway through the four-block business district, he stopped abruptly, his attention caught by a saloon on the opposite side of the street.

He studied the Granger Bar and Restaurant. There was something very familiar about the neat facade with its two front entrances and the combination of bar and dining room next door to each other. He stepped off the curb, pausing to let a dusty ranch pickup truck pass before he crossed the street. A red-and-white Help Wanted sign was taped inside the window to the left of the entry.

Maybe my luck is about to change, he thought. The small amount of cash in his pocket wouldn't last long, and he had yet to come up with a brilliant plan to learn his identity without chancing another attack from whoever wanted him dead.

The cool interior of the empty saloon was a welcome relief from the sweltering heat outside. Wooden booths with navy-blue vinyl upholstered benches lined two walls while round tables with seating for four were arranged haphazardly in the center of the room. At the back, an empty space in front of a raised stage clearly served as a dance floor. On his right was a bar that stretched the length of the wall, lined with mirrors that reached to the ceiling.

"Can I help you?"

A woman entered the room from a side door and walked toward him, skirting the tables. She carried a handful of red-and-white Help Wanted signs and a roll of Scotch tape.

A mane of pale-blond hair was pulled up into a ponytail, silky wisps escaping to curl against her nape. She wore a white tank top with narrow shoulder straps, her arms tan and smooth, while brief khaki shorts left her slender legs bare.

He stopped breathing. All his senses focused on her and the elusive feminine scent that reached his nostrils.

"Can I get you something? Anything?"

He realized he was staring at her mouth and when he snapped his attention higher, read wary concern in sea-green eyes framed by thick, dark lashes. Delicate dark brows arched questioningly above those fathomless eyes.

Lori Ashworth stared at the stranger, who stared back at her as if he'd been frozen in place.

He was tall, over six feet, with broad shoulders, lean hips and long legs. His black Western shirt had pearl snaps and was tucked into the waistband of faded Levis, a black leather belt with a conservative silver buckle threaded through the jeans' belt loops. Black cowboy boots covered his feet.

Faint beard stubble shadowed his jaw and cheeks, a shade darker than the mahogany tint of his hair. Beneath the arch of his brows, his eyes were thick-lashed and an unusual dark-gray color. On his right temple, near the hairline, perhaps five inches or so of white medical tape stood out starkly against tanned skin. The tape didn't quite cover a nasty-looking bump and a bruise that looked new and would no doubt be more defined and colorful by tomorrow.

He looked faintly rumpled and dangerous. And he oozed a sexual appeal that vibrated along her nerve endings.

She was sure she hadn't seen him before. He wasn't a man she would have forgotten. He was, however, the most interesting male to walk into her life in years, maybe ever.

She didn't know what he was doing in her bar but she'd definitely like him to stay for a while.

"Can I get you something to drink? A beer, maybe?" Fortunately, friendliness was expected from a bartender, she thought, and hopefully, he wouldn't realize the impact he was having on her.

"No, thanks, I don't drink alcohol."

His voice was deep, with a slight, lazy drawl that weakened her knees and stirred heat in her midsection.

"Well then, how about some ice water?"

A slow smile lifted the corners of his mouth. "Sounds good. I'd appreciate it."

He took a seat on one of the stools as Lori walked behind the bar. She filled a tall tumbler half full with ice and added water. "Here you go." She set the glass on a napkin and slid it across the counter in front of him.

She knew she was staring but couldn't look away from the rhythmic movement of the muscles in his throat as he swallowed.

The glass was empty when he set it back on the bar. He wiped the back of his hand over his lips, blotting a few drops of moisture.

Without comment, she refilled it and watched as he drained half the water before stopping.

"Thanks," he said.

"Not a problem. It's hot outside," she added.

His brief grin showed a flash of white teeth in his brown face. "Feels like it's over a hundred."

"No air-conditioning in your car?" she asked with sympathy.

"No car."

She gestured at the bandage on his temple. "What happened?"

"I was robbed."

She blinked, taken aback at the briefness of his reply. "What did they hit you with?"

"Something heavy." His wry tone was accompanied by a slight grin that lifted the corners of his mouth.

Lori was distracted by the sensual curve of his lips and he spoke again before she could gather her wits and question him further.

"Who do I see about the job?"

"That would be me—are you looking for work?" She gasped as she suddenly realized who this man was. Over six feet, dark hair, light eyes—he fit Bill's description perfectly, although his eyes were gray instead of light blue. But then, she knew for a fact that Bill was color blind. "Oh, my goodness! You're Troy Jones, aren't you! I was expecting you three days ago—Bill told me you were taking a week to go hiking in Yellowstone before you came to Granger." She looked again at the strip of white tape. "I'm guessing you're late because of the robbery?"

He nodded and took another drink of ice water.

"I was starting to worry about you. I tried to call Bill yesterday but he and Rhonda had already left for their cruise and since they'll be gone for a month, I didn't know who else to ask. I'm so relieved you're here—my late-shift bartender quit yesterday. Bill warned me you can only stay until the Four Buttes Saloon reopens in six weeks and told me he'd made you promise to return." She smiled with pleasure and relief and held out her hand. "I'm Lori Ashworth. I manage the bar and the restaurant next door."

He set the empty glass down and brushed his damp palm over his jeans-covered thigh. He had no idea how he knew beyond a doubt she was wrong about who he was. Neither did he have a clue as to what had become of the bartender the beautiful blonde had been expecting, but if she thought he was someone named Troy Jones and was willing to give him a job, he was more than glad to take it. The real Troy Jones would likely appear sooner or later but he'd handle that when it happened. For now he'd play the cards fate had dealt him.

He took her slim hand, registering the instant jolt of electricity and the feel of her soft, feminine palm in his. "It's a pleasure to meet you, Lori."

He didn't release her hand until she tugged slightly.

"Nice to meet you, too." A faint flush tinted her cheeks and her fingers weren't quite steady as she brushed a loose wisp of hair behind her ear. "How did you get to Granger without a car?"

"I hitched a ride with a trucker." He'd decided to stick with the story he'd told the driver. He had no memory of being robbed but it seemed logical to conclude that was why he'd landed in the ditch. "When they stole my car and gave me this—" he gestured at his temple "—they also took my wallet."

"I'm sorry." Her expression was sympathetic. "You can run a tab in the restaurant next door until you receive your first week's pay if you'd like. Since my family owns both businesses, it's not a problem. Just let the waitress know and we'll deduct the total from your check."

"I'll do that, thanks."

"Well…that's settled, then. I'll need to fill out the usual paperwork for a new hire, but we can put that off for a few days until you can replace your identification. We provide T-shirts stamped with our logo for all employees to wear while on duty and a room upstairs comes with the job. There's very little crime in Granger but every now and then teenagers break in and steal beer so we prefer to have someone living on the premises."

"Sounds good." He mentally raised his eyebrows when she quoted the salary and reined in the relief he felt at being offered somewhere to live. With his lack of finances, plus zero references, finding a rental would have been difficult.

"Great." She walked out from behind the bar. "Let me show you your new home."

They crossed the room and exited through an archway into a square hall. Lori paused to poke her head inside the open door of the restaurant's kitchen. "Ralph," she called. "I'm going upstairs for a few minutes—will you keep an eye on the bar?"

"No problem," a deep-bass voice replied.

"Thanks. I won't be long."

Just down the hall from the kitchen entry, a flight of stairs led upward. Lori started up the steps with Trey behind. Two treads below her, his taller height put his eyes at the level of her nape. Each step she climbed swung the silky length of her ponytail back and forth, brushing the bare skin above the tank top that ended at the dead center of her shoulder blades. There was something about

the way the thick swathe of pale hair kept in time
with the gentle sway of her hips that urged him to
reach out, wrap an arm around her waist, and pull
her back against him.

Fortunately they reached the landing at the top
of the stairs before he gave in to temptation.

"Here we are." Lori pushed open a door and
went inside.

Relieved by the diversion, Trey followed her
and realized that although she'd called it a "room"
earlier, it was actually a studio apartment. A
queen-size bed took up one corner, half-hidden
behind a waist-high bookcase divider that held a
TV. A small sofa sat against one wall, directly
opposite.

Upper and lower kitchen cabinets with a sink
and a small refrigerator made up a compact kitch-
en area where a coffeemaker and toaster sat on the
counter to the right of the stove. It was Spartan but
efficient.

"This is the bathroom." Lori leaned in to switch
on the light. "The washer and dryer are in the corner."

Trey caught a quick glimpse of a basic white
sink with a shower stall and the stacked appli-
ances.

"I had the place cleaned this morning and it has

everything you need." She slid open a closet door next to the bathroom. The tidy interior had drawers at one end, shelves in the center and a pole with hangers for clothing. "The bed linens and towels are stored in here."

She glanced around the apartment. "I hope you'll be comfortable. It's small and the cooking facilities are almost nonexistent. Most folks who stay here use the kitchen downstairs."

"So I can raid the restaurant's refrigerator at night if I want?" he asked.

"As long as the cook is okay with it. Ralph is particular about his kitchen. In fact," she said gravely, "he considers it his kingdom so I'd recommend you be very nice to him if you want to be allowed in there."

"Thanks for the heads-up," he responded, just as seriously. "I'll do that."

"Good." She gave the room a last look. "Well, I guess that's it. Your first shift is tonight from six p.m. to midnight. Saturday is normally our busiest night of the week but most of our customers will be at the rodeo in the next county this weekend. The annual celebration includes a beer garden and Nashville headliner entertainment so we don't have a band booked and we're closing early tonight. Kari and I will be working, too, so it's a good time for you to get used to the layout. I need to get back to work. Would you like to come with me and meet Ralph?"

"If he's the man I need to schmooze in order to get food, then I definitely want to meet him."

Dimples dented her cheeks when she laughed. "Have you eaten lunch?" she asked over her shoulder as he followed her back downstairs.

"No." *Nor breakfast and maybe not dinner last night either, judging by how hollow my stomach feels.*

"I'll introduce you to Ralph as soon as I check on the bar. We're not officially open for another fifteen minutes but sometimes locals drop in early."

The smell of roasting beef mixed with the tang of onion and barbecue sauce drifted out of the kitchen doorway as they passed. Trey's stomach rumbled. He hoped the bar was empty.

Unfortunately, it wasn't.

An older woman was perched on one of the blue upholstered stools, knees crossed and one backless high heel swinging. Her fingernails tapped an impatient tattoo on the polished surface of the counter.

"Where have you been, Lori?" Her voice was

sharp. "There was no one on duty when I came in. Anybody could have walked in off the street and emptied the cash register."

"There's no money in the till, Mom, or I wouldn't have left the door unlocked. I was upstairs, showing our new bartender the apartment." Lori's voice was even but Trey saw the subtle tightening around her mouth and the barely visible tensing of her body. "This is Troy Jones. Troy, this is my mother, Risa."

The older woman stared at him critically, not bothering to hide her negative assessment. "What happened to you?" She pointed at his head.

"Somebody hit me," he responded.

"Obviously," she said shortly. "The question is, were you starting the fight or were you stopping it?"

"I don't remember," he said honestly.

"Humph. We don't need a troublemaker," she said to her daughter, clearly dismissing him. "We need a man who'll help the bouncer stop fights, not start them."

"Troy was robbed, Mother," Lori replied. She rounded the end of the bar, took out a glass and poured ginger ale over ice for her mother. "That's how he got the bump."

"Robbed?" One dark brow winged upward. "Here in Granger?"

"No, ma'am," Trey said. "On the highway about a hundred miles south."

"Well, thank goodness it didn't happen here," Risa said. "Crime is rare in this town and we want it to stay that way."

Troy wondered with amusement if she blamed him for being robbed. Clearly, she wasn't going to forgive him for having been rapped on the head in the process.

Her gaze sharpened. "And what do you mean you don't remember?" she demanded. "Why don't you know what happened?"

"The doctor tells me I have some short-term memory loss caused by the blow to my head. One of the things I can't remember is what led up to my getting this cut and bump."

"Humph." She eyed him suspiciously. "So you staggered in here after getting clobbered and conned my daughter's sympathetic nature into giving you a job and a place to live?"

"Mother." Lori sounded exasperated. "He didn't stagger—he walks perfectly fine. And he's clearly an experienced bartender."

"How do you know?"

"Because he's been working at the Four Buttes Saloon, and Bill gave him a five-star recommendation. In fact, Bill says he's letting us borrow Troy only until his place is remodeled and then Bill made him promise to go back to work at the Four Buttes."

"Humph, he'll likely want to stay here. It's much nicer than that old place of Bill's." Risa sniffed. "And if he's as good as you apparently believe he is, we might want to keep him on."

"We'll see. I'm glad we've resolved the issue," Lori said with a wry smile. "I'll be back in a few minutes, I'm taking Troy next door to introduce him to Ralph."

"Don't be gone long," her mother said. "You know I don't wait on customers."

"Yes," Lori said dryly. "I know."

Troy nodded goodbye to Risa, but she'd already hopped down from her stool. Drink in one hand, she crossed the room to the jukebox. A moment later, the gravelly voice of Willy Nelson filled the saloon.

Ralph was a man with salt-and-pepper hair, black eyes and enough extra pounds on his five-ten frame to declare he enjoyed his own food. Trey took to him at first sight.

He also liked the kitchen with its overhead rack of gleaming pans. The big room, crowded with counters, huge grill, stove and baking ovens, resonated with a powerful feeling of familiarity and comfort. And the aromas wafting about made him realize he was beyond hungry.

"So, do you cook, Troy?" Ralph asked, continuing to knead bread dough on the flour-sprinkled counter.

Troy picked up a sharp knife, hefting the weight, and glimpsed a swift image of himself chopping scallions. "Do I cook?" he said slowly, testing the words. "I think I do."

"You think you do?" Ralph's dark eyebrows raised. "Don't you know?"

"Yeah," Trey said, more sure of himself. "I definitely cook."

"Good. When I need help, I'll draft you," Ralph said with satisfaction. "Like right now. Would you prep the chives, there on your left? They're going in the quiche for the Library Society brunch today. You can use the cutting board and drop them in the bowl."

"Sure." Trey washed his hands before placing a handful of chives on the board and beginning to chop.

"You don't know what you've started, Troy," Lori said, looking amused. "Ralph is a tyrant in the kitchen."

"Not true," Ralph quickly denied, his big hands deftly twisting and patting the dough before slipping it into bread pans. "I just don't have patience with incompetent help."

Lori rolled her eyes heavenward and laughed out loud. "And that covers ninety-nine percent of the people I hire."

"It's not easy to find good kitchen help," Ralph agreed with a chuckle. "But I can tell by the way our new bartender handles my knife that he knows what he's doing."

Startled, Trey realized he was wielding the sharp utensil with easy expertise and had reduced the bundle of chives to a bowlful of evenly cut pieces. *Good to know. Maybe I own a restaurant in my real life.*

"Be careful, Troy," Lori cautioned. "Or you'll find yourself working another shift for Ralph in here as well as your regular hours behind the bar."

"I wouldn't mind at all if I get to sample the food," he responded.

"That reminds me, Ralph. Troy hasn't had lunch. Can he raid the refrigerator?"

"Sure, he can eat in exchange for the chive chopping." Ralph winked at her.

"I'll leave you two, then," Lori said. "I haven't finished getting the bar ready to open. You'll be joining Kari and me a little before six tonight,

Troy. If you have any questions before then, I'm usually around."

"Thanks." Trey stared after her slim figure as she hurried out of the kitchen.

"She's quite a woman," Ralph commented.

Trey's gaze met the older man's shrewd, knowing eyes.

"I worked for her daddy before he died," Ralph continued. "Keeled over from a massive heart attack the year Lori graduated from college. She had big plans to work as a commercial artist in Chicago or New York, maybe Los Angeles. Instead, she came back to Granger and took over running this place so her kid sister and brother would have a decent life."

"What about her mother?" Troy asked. "Why didn't she take over the business?"

"Risa was hit hard by Doug's death—the whole family was, of course, but the kids were really worried about their mom. It's only in the last year she seems to be doing better. Plus, Risa never did have the temperament to manage a bar and restaurant. In fact, I'm pretty sure she would have sold out to the first bidder if Doug's will hadn't left the business to all four of them equally. The kids didn't want to sell and even if they had, the money wouldn't have lasted long."

Ralph slid the bread pans into the big ovens, then bent to lift a box of lettuce onto the counter. "Without Lori, the family would have been dead broke in six months and all of us would probably have been out of work. So you can see," he said, beginning to rinse the greens at the stainless steel sink, "why we're kinda protective of her." He eyed Trey. "Get my meaning?"

"Oh, yeah," Trey drawled. "Loud and clear."

"Good." Ralph nodded briskly. "You're welcome to raid the refrigerator, if you want. There's some prime rib left from last night if you're in the mood for a beef sandwich."

It appeared he'd passed some sort of test with Ralph, and Trey headed thankfully for the fridge.

The medication he'd taken at the clinic was wearing off by the time Trey left the kitchen and went upstairs to the apartment. His body ached all over and his head pounded, the site sore where the doctor had put in the row of stitches. The door was unlocked, the keys lying on the counter. He took down a glass from the cabinet and filled it at the kitchen tap, tossing two more pain pills down his throat and chasing them with cold water.

Fortunately, the apartment had a small window-mounted air conditioner that was sufficient to cool the place to a bearable temperature.

He stripped off his clothes and turned on the shower. After he scrubbed thoroughly, he let the spray beat against the tender muscles in his shoulders and back until the water went cold.

Then he dried off, threw all his clothes into the washer and padded naked into the main room. The linens on the bed were blessedly cool and fresh; he set the alarm for 3:00 p.m. and crawled between the sheets. He was asleep almost as soon as his head hit the pillow.

When the buzzer went off, he dragged himself out of bed but he had to splash cold water on his face before he was truly awake. By four o'clock his clothes were dry and he was back downstairs. He stopped in the kitchen doorway.

"Hey, Ralph."

The burly chef glanced up. "Hey, yourself."

Trey strolled into the kitchen, carefully skirting the busy crew at the long center counter. "Any chance I can get something to eat?"

"Sure." Ralph pointed his knife at the stool shoved beneath the counter at the quiet end. "Have a seat. Are you particular or do you want a plate of the house special?"

"What's the house special?"

"Prime rib with garlic mashed potatoes, almond green beans and a small dinner salad."

Trey's stomach growled with anticipation. "I'll have the special."

"Good choice." Ralph gestured one of his assistants closer. "Mary, get Troy here an order of the prime rib, will you. And something to drink—what do you want, Troy?"

"Ice water will be perfect." He smiled at the middle-aged woman. Moments later, she set a steaming plate in front of him, followed in quick succession by a salad bowl, cutlery wrapped in a snowy-white napkin, and a stemmed water glass.

She nodded at his murmured thanks and left him to eat.

Seated at one end of the big kitchen, Trey could observe without being intrusive, which suited him just fine. He wanted to know as much as possible about the people he'd be working with, especially Ralph. He'd instinctively liked the chef. Watching him deal with his assistants further confirmed Trey's original assessment that Ralph was shrewd, efficient, firm without being obnoxious, and clearly respected by his staff.

And a hell of a good cook.

By four-thirty, Trey had finished eating, thanked Ralph, and left the busy kitchen. He walked next door and took a seat at one end of the long bar.

"Afternoon. What can I get you?" The middle-aged man behind the bar had a pleasant face and graying hair.

"Just ice water, thanks."

"I haven't seen you in here before," the bartender said as he set a glass in front of Trey. "You new in town?"

"As of this morning—and I start work here tonight."

"No kidding—you must be the guy Lori's been expecting for the last few days."

"That's right. Troy Jones." He held out his hand.

"Butch Roth." He shook Trey's hand and grinned, gesturing around the quiet room. "You picked a good day to start. It's always pretty empty during rodeo weekend."

"That's what Lori said. I thought I'd come in early and hang around, sort of get the feel of the crowd."

"Good plan." Butch nodded sagely. "You won't have any trouble with the customers. We get a good mix of ranchers and townsfolk in here, nice people."

"Is this the only bar in town?" Trey asked.

"We're the only one with a first-class restaurant and Saturday-night entertainment," Butch replied. "There's a tavern out near the highway but it's small and caters to a different crowd."

"Oh, yeah. I think Bill might have mentioned it—is it called the Bull 'n' Bash?" Trey pretended to take a drink of water but he watched Butch's face with sharp interest.

"Nope. The Blue Moon. Been there since the fifties and it looks like nobody's painted it since the year it was built." Butch smiled and shook his head. "We should go there some night, if you've a hankering for rough company and a guaranteed bar brawl."

"No, thanks." Trey laughed and the two chatted casually for a while until Butch was called away by a young couple seated farther down the polished bar.

So the Bull 'n' Bash named in the mysterious letter isn't in Granger. Disappointed, Trey sipped his water, swinging around on the seat to study the room. A wide doorway at the far end of the room opened into a space where he could see several pool tables.

That looks familiar. He instinctively knew he played pool. Unfortunately, he couldn't remember where. But his gut also told him he was good at it.

He scanned the saloon. A neon sign advertising Moosehead lager hung above the archway leading to the hall and the restaurant beyond, while a trophy-size deer head with an impressive rack of antlers dominated the wall near the exit. So many things about the bar's interior felt familiar to him—from the deer's antlers and the green felt on the pool tables to the amber glass in the beer sign, the throaty bass of the jukebox and the gleaming countertop.

He checked out what he could see of the long alley behind the bar where Butch was currently the sole employee. It, too, felt comfortable. So did the wooden rack above the well that held various sizes of stemmed glassware, hung upside down and easily accessible from below.

He sipped his ice water and eavesdropped while customers asked Butch for drinks, making his own mental list of ingredients and mixing rules. Then he watched Butch fill the orders for margaritas, Long Island iced teas, Acapulco Zombies, frozen daiquiris, MacNaughton's on the rocks, and a long roster of other cocktails.

By the time six o'clock arrived and Kari and Lori joined him to relieve Butch, Trey was convinced he'd worked as a bartender sometime in his past. The fixings necessary to make mixed drinks seemed to be recorded on one of his memory chips that still worked. He was confident he could get through the next few hours without Lori discovering his secret—the knowledge was a huge relief. He wasn't ready to let anyone learn how little he knew about his past.

When he looked up and saw Lori, he felt the same jolt of pure lust that he'd felt earlier in the day. She'd changed into a pair of jeans, a scoop-necked white T-shirt and thick-soled sandals. A chunk of turquoise wrapped in a spiral of thin gold wire hung on a chain around her neck, and a matching stone bracelet circled her wrist.

Her platinum hair was still in a ponytail, the ends brushing her shoulders each time she turned her head.

The bar wasn't crowded but there was a slow, steady stream of customers until nearly ten o'clock, when a general exodus began. By ten-thirty, the big room was nearly empty. Despite having eavesdropped on as many conversations as possible, Trey hadn't heard anything that keyed any recall in him. He busied himself with wiping down the already gleaming bar surface while he listened to Lori and Kari discuss the latter's upcoming wedding.

Clearly a longtime friend of Lori's, Kari was a curvy redhead who flirted as naturally as she breathed. When she turned to him and announced she was engaged to the only good guy in town, he had to smile.

"How long have you known him?" he asked, drawn into the conversation despite himself.

"Since we were in grade school." She transferred fresh lemons into the refrigerated case and grinned impishly. "It took a while to convince him marriage is a good idea."

"Yeah, like ten years," Lori said dryly. She stood at the register, counting cash and change.

"Ten is better than twenty," Kari replied blithely. "Besides, Mason is worth waiting for."

"I can't argue with that," Lori agreed. "Mason really is a great guy," she said to Trey. "But he's the shy type, always has been, and we've known each other since the first day of kindergarten."

"That's one of the benefits of growing up in a small town—you have years to get to know people," Trey commented. *It's interesting they've lived here all their lives but they didn't recognize me. Pretty conclusive evidence that I'm not from this area.* It also might mean the cryptic letter he'd found in the ditch wasn't his, he realized, which would effectively eliminate his only clue to what happened. Neither brought him any closer to solving his identity problem. But on the other hand, maybe it meant he was safe in Granger because if he hadn't lived or worked here, whoever robbed and tried to kill him might not know to look for him in the small town.

"Yes, that's the good news—and the bad news," Lori was saying with a shrug.

"Bad news?" He forced his attention back to the two women. "What could be bad about spending a lot of time with someone before marrying?"

"That's the good part of the equation," she agreed. "But the bad half is that we've all known each other since we were practically babies. Where's the mystery? For instance, I remember when Mason got sick in first grade and lost his lunch all over the teacher's shoes. Hard to forget that and see him as Kari's answer to Romeo."

The expression of revulsion on her face was priceless. Trey laughed. "I see what you mean." He slotted clean glasses into the rack above the bar.

"Your problem is that you have too good a memory, Lori," Kari put in. "And you're too cynical."

"Cynical?" Trey lifted an eyebrow, intrigued by the word.

"She thinks men and monogamy are incompatible. I keep telling her she needs to meet someone like Mason and develop a new perspective." Kari tossed the last comment over her shoulder as she left to tend to a customer at the opposite end of the bar.

"You don't believe men can be monogamous?" he asked.

"I suppose there must be men somewhere who are capable of being faithful." Lori finished rinsing a glass and dried it with efficient ease. "But all those I've met, except for Mason and my brother, haven't been."

Before he could respond, she picked up a damp towel and handed him another. "Let's wipe off the tables."

She clearly didn't want to discuss the subject further. She also hadn't named her father in the short list of men she trusted. He wondered why.

I'm not going to ask, he thought. He needed to stay focused on learning who he was and keeping a low profile until he did. Lori Ashworth was a distraction he didn't need and couldn't afford.

They left Kari to tend to the sparse group of two older couples and one lone cowboy seated at the long bar.

"Quiet night," he commented as they worked their way around the empty room.

"Yes." Lori straightened, tucking her hair behind her ear. "We'll probably close early if it doesn't pick up by eleven. And you can sleep in tomorrow morning."

He nodded, thinking he'd spend the day at the local library, assuming there was one. With luck, it would have a public access computer and Internet service.

Kari joined them and began to wipe off a nearby table. "Bye now," she called to the two couples as they walked toward the exit.

Trey realized the cowboy had disappeared, too, and the three of them were the only people left in the spacious saloon.

"You're coming to the ball game Monday night, aren't you, Troy?" Kari asked.

He would if it increased his chances of discovering something about his past, he thought. If not, he'd give it a pass. "I noticed the poster on the wall," he said, without really answering her question. "Does the bar sponsor a team?"

Lori nodded. "The Granger Blue Jays. We're tied for first place in our league—and Monday evening at eight o'clock we have a home game at the field in City Park."

"You definitely should come," Kari said. "It's lots of fun, and the local restaurants take turns staffing the food stand. Ralph's doing it Monday and he's making barbecued ribs."

"That alone means you shouldn't miss the game," Lori said with a smile. "No one makes ribs like Ralph."

"And his pulled pork is even better," Kari assured him. "Much better—Ralph is king of the barbecue."

"Our team has the late slot, so the game doesn't start until eight, but if you wait until then to get there, the food might be gone," Lori said. "The early game starts at five and a lot of fans eat their dinner at the park."

"If your team's tied for first place, you should have a good turnout," Trey commented.

"Everyone for miles around will be there," Lori said. "Granger loves baseball."

"I see." Satisfied with the information, Trey decided he'd go to the game. But he'd find a place to observe the crowd without being seen. Maybe he'd get lucky and spot someone whose face and name he knew.

And if I don't, and if no one recognizes me,

either, at least I'll know I can probably hide in Granger until my memory comes back.

He hoped to hell the doctor's assessment was right and his amnesia cleared up within a few weeks. He didn't think he was going to be good at pretending to be someone he wasn't. The only advantage he had was that no one in Granger seemed to know the real Troy Jones.

At least, no one he'd met so far.

The intercom in Harlan Kerrigan's office in Wolf Creek buzzed. Impatient at the interruption, he flicked the switch.

"What?" he snapped.

"You have a call from your son on line two, sir."

He didn't bother acknowledging his secretary. Instead, he turned off the intercom and picked up the receiver.

"Yes?"

"I just had a phone call from Bobby Rimes."

"Did he get the letter from Trey Harper?"

"No…"

Harlan uttered a string of curses, his frustration exploding in anger. "Why the hell not?"

"Evidently Carl hit Harper a little too hard."

Harlan clenched his teeth and drew a deep

breath. "Explain," he demanded, his voice clipped with the effort to keep from yelling.

"Bobby and Carl followed Trey when he left town on Friday. There was an accident south of here and traffic backed up until the troopers could clear the road. Trey walked to a nearby motel office where the clerk was handing out free coffee and while he was there, Bobby punctured one of his tires—just enough for a slow leak. Then they followed Harper and pulled up behind him when he stopped to fix the flat tire. That's when Carl hit him with a tire iron."

"Is he dead?"

"They think so."

"What did they do with the body?"

"Threw it in a ditch north and east of here along the highway."

"And Harper's car? What did they do with that?"

"Bobby says they left it in a rancher's quarry, well off the road."

"So Harper's dead and they didn't find the letter," Harlan said slowly.

"Apparently Carl searched his pockets and took everything, but there was no sign of the letter."

"Hell." Harlan thought a moment. "Where are the Rimes brothers now?"

"Just across the line in Wyoming."

"Send them some money and tell them to stay there until they hear from me."

"Do you want me to pay a visit to the O'Connell woman and get the photos?"

"No," Harlan exploded. "I don't want you anywhere near Sherry or the town of Granger. I want to keep a lid on this."

"Sure, Dad. Will do."

Harlan hung up the receiver and glared at the phone.

Idiots, he thought. *I'm surrounded by idiots.* He needed that letter. He hadn't believed Sherry O'Connell would follow through with her threat to blackmail him but apparently, she had. Bribing the postmistress to let him know if either Trey or Raine Harper received a letter from Sherry had been easy, but he hadn't dared ask her to give it to him.

It should have been a simple thing for Bobby and Carl to rob Trey and recover the letter. Unfortunately, it appeared they'd killed him in the attempt, and still hadn't retrieved the letter.

Now all I can do is pretend I don't know what

happened to Trey Harper while keeping tabs on the search for him that's sure to follow.

He hated loose ends. They annoyed the hell out of him.

Chapter Three

Before noon on Monday, he walked to Granger's small library, waiting in the shade of a spreading elm until the doors were unlocked. The compact building boasted public Internet access and two computers. Trey claimed one and spent the afternoon surfing the Net, hunting for any information about the Bull 'n' Bash. He was convinced the meeting place referenced in the mysterious letter must be a bar, but unfortunately, he didn't find a thing.

He also scanned online newspapers for Billings, Helena, Missoula and Butte, but found no reports of a missing person whose description matched his own. The search was slow and ponderous because the library didn't have high-speed service. By the time the librarian told him she was closing at 5:00 p.m., his eyes were dry and itchy from staring at the small green screen and his right hand was cramped from clicking the mouse. He left, planning to return the next day and continue looking.

The building was quiet when he let himself in through the restaurant's alley door and the aroma of barbecue sauce hung in the air in the kitchen.

Ralph must have done prep work for his famous ribs here, he thought, as he raided the refrigerator. Carrying a thick ham sandwich and an ice-cold soda, he climbed the stairs to the apartment. A bag containing a half-dozen T-shirts in white, navy and black hung on the doorknob and he carried it inside, tossing it on the bed. Nice of the boss to provide company shirts since he only had one of his own.

He set the soda and sandwich next to the sofa and switched on the TV. The early-evening news droned through the weather report, predicting more sunshine and hot temperatures. He sat on the couch and stretched out his legs, propping his boots on the small coffee table while he ate. Despite watching the channel for an hour, he didn't learn anything that jogged his absent memory.

Frustrated, he turned off the set. The clock on the kitchen microwave told him it was nearly 8:00 p.m.

Time to head for the ball field.

The crowd noise was audible as soon as he stepped onto the sidewalk downtown and grew louder as he walked the few blocks to the game. Evening was slipping toward dusk, the light taking on a mellow golden hue.

The baseball field filled one end of the park, flanked by wooden bleachers, six rows high, with a small refreshment stand at the end. Trey entered the recreational area at the other end, where tall old maple trees shaded walkways, a few picnic tables and a grouping of children's playground equipment. He chose a spot beneath the spreading limbs of an oak and leaned against the trunk, studying the scattered groups of people dotting the stretch of grassy lawn between the tree and the baseball diamond. Some were family groups with children, some were couples, all sat or sprawled on blankets.

He studied the faces of the adults as they chatted and dealt with the kids racing about. None of them looked familiar. His location allowed him to scan the crowd seated in the bleachers, too. Anyone watching him would have thought he was following the game, but in reality all his attention was on the sea of faces.

Again he didn't recognize a single person, male or female, adult or child, packing the white wooden structure. The field lights came on, their brightness a sharp contrast to the earlier mellow gold light. Trey realized the sun had dropped below the horizon while he'd been intent on studying faces, and dusk had edged shadows beneath the tree where he stood.

He didn't come. The bubble of anticipation Lori had felt since Saturday night had burst, replaced by disappointment. Resolutely she made a mental list of all the reasons why she shouldn't care if Troy had decided to give the game a miss. *He's only here for a few weeks. Just because the Blue Jays' games are a big deal to us doesn't mean they are to him. Maybe he doesn't even like baseball. Kari and I never asked him if he did, we just assumed he was interested.*

She left Ralph packing the last of his equipment at the refreshment stand and walked toward the bleachers to rejoin Kari.

"Hey, Lori!"

She paused, searching the groups of people seated on blankets in the grassy area past the baseball grounds. A woman waved, claiming her attention, and she angled away from the ball diamond and toward her.

"Hi, Patty." She ruffled the hair of her friend's three-year-old son. "Are you enjoying the game, Nathan?"

"Yes! I'm the best batter in the world!" He grinned at her and raced away with another little boy.

"Excellent," Lori said to his mother, laughing. "Good to know you're training the next generation of Team Blue Jay."

"So far, he can't even hit a wiffle ball, but he's trying," his dad said with a smile. "I'd better go grab him before he races blocks from here. Nice to see you, Lori."

"You, too, Jared. How have you been, Patty?"

Lori chatted with her friend for a few moments before saying goodbye. As she turned away, she glanced idly over the clusters of people spread over the grass and then to the widely spaced trees.

A man stood under one of the oaks. Her gaze moved past him, then snapped back. Even in the deepening dusk, she recognized the distinctive broad shoulders and long legs.

She switched direction and crossed the park toward him.

He leaned against the tree, one shoulder braced against the rough bark of the trunk, arms crossed over his chest. His white T-shirt was one of the company shirts she'd left outside his apartment door. The familiar block letters spelled out Granger Bar and Restaurant above a small silhouette of a bronc rider just over his heart. Tucked into the waistband of his jeans, the short sleeves leaving powerful biceps bare, the simple shirt she'd seen a dozen men wear suddenly took on a whole new look.

"Hello. I thought you'd decided not to come. Have you been here long?"

"Long enough to know your team is good."

"They are, aren't they?" She forced herself to stop studying his body and looked at the field, where a lanky blond man, his baseball cap turned backward, had just stepped up to bat. "That's Mason, Kari's fiancé."

"Can he hit?" Trey asked.

Before Lori could reply, Mason swung and connected and the crowd was on its feet, screaming encouragement as he sped toward first base, rounded second and third and pounded toward home. He lost the race with the ball when he slid into home base and the umpire yelled "out."

Lori planted her hands on her hips and glared at the ball field. "He was safe by a mile," she shouted. "Did you see that?" she demanded, turning to Trey.

He grinned at her, his teeth a slash of white in the dusk. "I did. And, yes, he was safe. Bad call by the ump."

She narrowed her eyes at him suspiciously. "Are you really agreeing with me?"

"Hey." He threw up his hands in surrender. "I never argue with a woman about her team."

"That doesn't mean you agree with me."

"Not always, but in this instance, I do. Your friend was home. The ump needs glasses."

She grinned. "Excellent! Let's go join Kari in the bleachers—we can cheer for Mason and tell her the umpire must be blind."

He hesitated, and for a moment she thought he was going to refuse, but then he shrugged.

"Sure, why not."

Nerves prickled, her nape tingling with awareness as he climbed the bleachers behind her. She inched her way past fans to reach the open spot beside Kari.

"Did you see that call?" Kari demanded. "Hi, Troy."

"Yes, we did," Lori said.

"Evenin'," Trey drawled at the same moment.

"…and we agree, Mason was robbed," Lori finished.

"He certainly was." Kari glared at the field, where the opposing team was at bat. "That umpire's been favoring the other team all night."

The game continued, with Lori and Kari filling Trey in on the strengths, weaknesses, and history of the players. The score was tied at the end of the ninth and the game went into extra innings, the crowd on the edge of its seat when Mason came up to bat once more.

"Come on, Mason!" Kari yelled.

He swung and missed twice. Lori groaned and held her breath. The third swing slugged the ball and the fans rose to their feet with a roar.

"Home run! It's a home run!" Kari shrieked, grabbing Lori's arm and jumping up and down. All around them, people were screaming, the noise and excitement deafening as they yelled and grabbed their neighbors in bear hugs. Without giving it a thought, Lori threw her arms around Trey and kissed him.

The kiss was more an exuberant release of emotion than sexual, and for a split second he stood totally still. Then he enfolded her in his arms and kissed her back and, just as quickly, it became something else entirely.

The celebrating crowd around them faded, she couldn't hear the noise. Pressed against him from chest to thigh, she was swamped by the feel of his hard, powerful male body, the strength of his embrace and the heated pressure of his mouth on hers.

Then it was over. He released her and stepped back. She swayed, disoriented, and he caught her forearm, steadying her. She looked into his eyes and thought she saw the same shocked awareness that filled her, but then the shutters came down and she couldn't read any emotion there at all.

Kari pulled her around and hugged her. Lori staggered, still feeling dizzy, but Kari didn't appear to notice.

"We won! And Mason got the winning hit! How cool is that?" Kari crowed. "Come on. Let's go congratulate him."

People were pouring out of the bleachers and

onto the field. Kari tugged Lori after her. She glanced over her shoulder and saw Trey join the throng heading for the celebration below them. Reassured he wasn't being excluded and left behind, she concentrated on descending the bleachers without tripping amid the jostling crowd.

Unfortunately, when they reached the playing field and she could look about her, he was nowhere in sight.

What did that kiss mean? She'd been carried away by celebrating and started it, but then he'd taken over. And he'd been the one to end it. She'd been so lost in the feeling, she'd forgotten they were standing in plain sight of most of Granger.

I shouldn't have kissed her. Trey lay in bed, hands stacked beneath his head, staring at the ceiling. Midnight had come and gone. It was more than three hours since he'd left Lori at the ball field and he couldn't stop thinking about her.

She'd caught him off guard, he thought. And he was sure the exuberant hug and kiss were only a reaction to the moment. She'd been swept up in the excitement of winning the game.

But there was nothing innocent about her

response when she'd kissed him back. She'd been a willing participant.

If she'd been any more willing, they would have set the bleacher on fire. He shifted restlessly. Just remembering how she felt, curves pressed against him, the hot silk of her mouth beneath his.

Damn.

He couldn't get involved with her. When she found out he'd lied to her about being Troy Jones, she was going to be mad as hell. And she'd find out. The real Troy Jones could walk into the Granger Bar any day. The longer he stayed here and pretended to be Jones, the more likely it was he'd be caught.

If he let the attraction go any further, she'd hate his guts when she learned the truth.

I have to stay away from her. And just how was he going to do that while she was his boss? he wondered. He had no idea.

Avoiding Lori turned out to be easier than he'd expected. Her normal working hours, he learned, were from 8:00 a.m. to 5:00 p.m. She'd only worked alongside Kari on his first night because he was new.

So the rest of the week he pretended to sleep late each morning, then got a bagged lunch and spent his afternoons on the Internet at the library. He didn't return to the bar until after 5:00 p.m. to work his evening shift.

He kept his eyes and ears open and netted a lot of information about the town of Granger and its residents, but no clues as to his own identity. Not a single person seemed to recognize him, and no one acted the slightest bit skeptical or taken aback when he told them his name was Troy Jones.

Which, by the way, was beginning to grate on his nerves. Since Troy Jones wasn't his real name, each time someone called him Troy, the sense of it being almost, but not quite, right was driving him crazy.

His daily headaches had stopped but he suffered occasional severe, stabbing pains in his temple. Usually this followed his efforts to recall something after an unexpected, vivid flash of memory. The resulting frustration had him gritting his teeth when the brief glimpse didn't unleash a flood of memories.

In fact, frustration had become his daily companion, and he was starting to question whether he should talk to the local sheriff after all. But his instinctive caution always won out.

The weekend came and went, and on Monday just before noon, he let himself into his apartment after paying a visit to the clinic. Dr. Reese had removed the stitches and pronounced him healed, but when told about the ongoing memory loss, hadn't been able to offer anything helpful. Beyond saying it was encouraging that he was having flashbacks, his only advice was to give it time.

Time, Trey thought with disgust. How much time was it going to take before he remembered everything? Hell, he'd settle for only one or two pieces of real information, like his name or address.

Someone knocked on the door, interrupting his brooding.

"Hey, Troy, you in there? You've got a phone call."

He yanked open the door. Startled, the busboy outside hastily retreated several steps.

"Lori wants to talk to you on the kitchen phone."

He followed the kid downstairs and picked up the receiver of the wall phone just inside the kitchen door. "Hello," he said cautiously.

"I'm sorry to bother you on your day off, Troy, but I have an emergency. I asked Ralph if he could rescue me, but he said the restaurant is too busy for him to leave right now, and he suggested I talk to you. Do you know anything about plumbing? Please say you do. I have water all over my kitchen floor, the plumber is out of town, and I'm desperate."

She really did sound flustered, he thought. Surely he could keep his distance and his hands off her for an hour or two.

"Where do you live?"

Chapter Four

"**I**'m so grateful you could come and help me this afternoon," Lori said as she led him through the living room and into the kitchen.

"No problem." He stopped, surveying the room. The tile floor gleamed wetly, and a pile of saturated towels was dumped in one side of the double sink. The doors to the cabinet below were open wide, the contents crammed into a nearby bucket, a jumble of bottles of cleaning products, sponges and brushes. "What happened?"

"I have no idea. I switched on the dishwasher

and left the room for a few minutes. When I came
back, water was pouring out from under it and the
sink. I managed to get the water valve turned off
but I'm afraid that's the extent of my plumbing expertise." She eyed him anxiously. "Ralph said it
sounded like a hose to the dishwasher might have
broken. What do you think?"

"I think he might be right." He sat on his heels
and examined the pipes beneath the sink. "Have
you got tools?"

"Dad's are in the garage."

An hour later, Trey twisted the pipe wrench for
the final time. He lay on his back on the floor with
his head and shoulders in the cupboard, an array
of plumbing gizmos whose use Lori could only
guess at on the floor next to his hips and legs.

"There, that should do it." He slid out from
beneath the sink, tested the water faucet, then
started the dishwasher.

When several moments passed and nothing
more exciting happened than the steady hum of the
machine, Lori grinned with delight. "It works!"

"Yes, ma'am," he said. He picked up the bucket
filled with cleaning items. "Do you want these
stored under the sink?"

"Yes, please." While he sat on his heels and

tidied them away, Lori plucked the wet towels from the sink and disappeared into the utility room. Within seconds she was back.

"I don't have champagne to celebrate surviving my flooded kitchen but I do have some of Ralph's carrot cake in the fridge."

"I'm always ready for cake," he replied easily, smiling at her. Her gaze dropped to his mouth and a faint pink stained her cheekbones. As surely as if he could read her mind, he knew she was remembering that kiss. He nearly reached for her.

"Excellent," she said brightly, turning away to take a plastic container from the fridge and slice cake onto plates before collecting forks from a drawer. "All I have to drink is bottled water and ginger ale, but I can make coffee."

"Water works for me."

"Good. Would you snag two bottles out of the fridge for us?"

She led the way onto the screened-in lanai and set the cake plates atop a round wicker table. Trey handed her one of the bottles and dropped into a chair beside her.

"I really appreciate your help. I'm sure this isn't the way you'd planned to spend your day off," she said, unscrewing the bottle cap.

"No, but the library will still be there tomorrow."

"The library?" She sipped water and eyed him with interest. "I wouldn't have pegged you for a man who spends his free time in the library."

"Hey, I read," he protested, earning a smile from her. "Actually, I've been using their computer to browse the Internet for anything that might jog my memory."

"Oh, I see." She took a bite of cake and chewed thoughtfully. "I know it's none of my business, and I don't mean to pry, but just how bad is your amnesia?"

"I don't have total recall," he said, purposely vague. "But the doc tells me my memory will come back, eventually."

"That must be reassuring," she said. "I can't imagine how difficult it would be not to remember everything. I think waiting for it to return would drive me crazy. Does it bother you?"

"I think you could say it bothers me," he said dryly.

"Poor you." Sympathy colored her tone and warmed her expressive features. "Did the doctor say if you can expect to have your memory return suddenly? Or will you recall bits and pieces over time until you know everything about your past?"

"I think he believes I'll slowly recover all my memories, not in a flood, but more like a trickle."

"It's too bad Bill and Rhonda aren't home. I'm sure they could give you details that would help fill in gaps in your history. Unfortunately, their cruise lasts at least a month. But—" her face brightened "—what about the other people you worked with in Four Buttes? Surely your friends could give you information?"

He shrugged, stalling for time so he could come up with a plausible reason not to agree with her suggestion. "They could, if they were home. But everybody working for Bill scattered the morning after he closed the bar for remodeling. We all wanted to take advantage of the long break and nobody planned to return until just before we had to go back to work."

"Oh." She frowned. "That's too bad. It does seem every possible avenue is closed, at least temporarily, doesn't it? If there's anything I can do to help, please let me know."

"Are you serious?" he asked, studying her features and seeing only genuine concern.

"Absolutely," she said. "In fact…" She sat up straighter. "I know the library's Internet service is slow as a slug—my brother complains loud and long when he's home and has to use it. But I have access in my office and it's fast, really fast, compared to the library's."

"That's nice of you, Lori, but I don't want to invade your space while you're working."

"No, I insist. You won't be in my way. I use the computer on my desk and have a laptop connected to the Internet on a second desk. You can use it anytime during office hours, which usually means between nine in the morning and five or six at night, depending on what's happening in the restaurant."

She was clearly determined. He gave in, though he doubted he'd actually take her up on the offer. The more he was around her, the better he liked the person inside the outer package of curves, silky hair and lush lips. Though he thought it was unlikely, he had no clue if he had a girlfriend, a fiancée or even a wife somewhere. He needed to keep his distance from Lori until he knew for sure. "As long as it won't inconvenience you, then, thanks."

"Good, that's settled. I'll trade you use of my laptop for your help today."

"I would have done it for free." He lifted a forkful of cake with cream cheese frosting. "Being paid with Internet access and cake is better than union wages."

She laughed. "Have you worked as a plumber, too?"

"Not that I know of."

"Oh. I thought…" She shrugged. "When you mentioned union wages, I thought perhaps you had experience with a plumbers' union."

"No, that's just something my dad used to say. And he wasn't a plumber either."

"What did he do, your dad?"

"He owned a bar and restaurant," Trey responded absentmindedly, mesmerized by the sweep of her tongue as she licked a bit of white frosting from her bottom lip.

Clearly surprised, she stopped eating to stare at him. "So that's why you're so good with our customers."

"Yeah. Probably." Where the hell did that come from? Distracted by the information, Trey probed the memory, trying to unravel more details.

"Was your dad's place here in Montana? I wonder if he knew my father? Maybe they belonged to the Restaurant Guild at the same time." Lori leaned forward, clearly intrigued, the plate in front of her forgotten.

"I don't know. The only thing I remember is a dinner table with the family sitting around it and all of us laughing at a story he'd told us about what happened at work that day."

"Did he say what he did at work?" She waved her hand. "I mean, did he talk about cooking as if he were a chef?"

"No. I didn't actually hear him speak." He searched for the words to explain. "It was more that I just…knew."

"Who were the other people at the table?"

Unaware that he was doing so, Trey massaged the back of his neck, where tense pain was building. "Mom, Dad, myself and two other kids. That's all."

A faint frown drew a vee between her brows. "You're getting a headache, aren't you?"

Surprised, he instantly stopped rubbing his nape and picked up his fork. "A small one, nothing to worry about. How long have you lived in Granger?" He changed the subject abruptly. He didn't want to tell her any more lies, nor did he want her to know how little he recalled of his past.

She hesitated, as if she wanted to say more, but then settled back in her chair in a gesture of acquiescence. "All my life. I grew up in this house." Her gaze moved over the sunny backyard. "I never thought I'd still be living here. It's funny how life turns out. I didn't plan to come back to Granger after college but I do enjoy running the businesses. There's always a challenge of some sort."

"Like bartenders not showing up on time?" he asked.

She laughed. "Yes, that does happen on occasion and it's definitely challenging."

"And the house?" He gestured at the backyard. "All the gardening and maintenance that goes with a house—pressure washing the roof, cleaning gutters, painting walls—you like doing all that?"

"I don't actually *do* all the work by myself," she said mildly. "But yes, I enjoy taking care of my home."

"Your home?" he said, curious. "I assumed it belonged to your mother since you said you live here with her."

"Mom and I are sharing, but Dad's will left it to all four of us—me, Mom and my younger sister and brother, Jane and Randy. I suppose I refer to it as 'my' home because I'm the one taking care of it at the moment."

"What happens if one of you gets married? Does the new husband move in or does the couple sell their share and buy a house somewhere else?"

She frowned, puzzled. "Hmm. You know, I

haven't thought of that. I have no idea. Not that I expect to need an answer anytime soon. Jane and Randy still have several years of college to finish and my mother…well, she dates occasionally but I can't see her getting married."

"Why not?"

"I don't think marriage is on her agenda. She's still trying to adjust to being a widow." Her mouth had a sad curve.

Trey was silent. Lori seemed to be struggling with her dad's death, too.

"I don't know if Mom will ever get over Dad leaving us. In some ways I think she's angry at him. Before he died, he worked long hours, as most business owners do, and they often argued about him being away from home so much." She looked away.

Trey's gaze followed hers, out across the lawn to the fence marking the boundary line. A climbing rose tumbled over the pickets in a blanket of pink blooms and glossy green leaves. "Everybody grieves in their own way," he said. "I expect she'll move past the anger sooner or later." He knew with sudden conviction that he, too, was well acquainted with grief.

"Yes, that's what all the counselors have told us."

She glanced at him, her eyes dark. Then she blinked and he wondered if he'd imagined the sadness and vulnerability in the moss-green depths. She pushed back her chair and stood.

"Ralph told me you asked him about the history connected to the carved wood frames round the mirrors behind the bar. If you'd like to come into the office, I'll show you Dad's collection of Granger memorabilia, especially the pieces from the family business. A local artist built our bar with mahogany logged in Belize by descendants of Caribbean pirates—four of them arrived with the shipment of wood and stayed to help with the construction. My great-grandfather took photos of the work when it was underway in the early 1900s."

He strolled after her into the house and down the hall to a small office. She clearly didn't want to talk about her father's death, nor her mother's grief. And probably not her own, either, he thought.

The hallway had floor-to-ceiling windows on one side and the opposite wall was hung with drawings framed in narrow black. Sunlight poured in, highlighting the pen-and-ink sketches behind the glass.

Trey slowed, drawn to the bold black ink caricatures of people he recognized from the Granger Bar.

"These are really good. This is Kari, isn't it? And this is Ralph?" He bent closer. "They look a lot younger."

"They are." Lori joined him, hands tucked into her shorts pockets. "I drew those while I was still in high school."

"Where's your recent work?" he asked, stepping back to scan the length of the wall, expecting to find current drawings of Kari and Ralph.

"There isn't any. I stopped sketching a few years ago."

"You stopped? Why?"

"I don't have time anymore. The restaurant and bar take most of my days, and what little free time I have is eaten up with other obligations." She shrugged. "Too much work, not enough time. That's the story of my life."

"I thought artists this good kept creating, no matter what else was going on in their lives."

"That's the generally held belief. Unfortunately, my version of the story is a little different."

"Don't you miss it?"

The naked yearning on her face appeared and

was gone so quickly, Trey would have missed the emotion if he hadn't been totally focused on her.

"It was a dream. I don't have time for that nonsense anymore."

"No one should give up dreaming," he said with conviction. "And it's downright criminal for someone with your talent not to use it."

"Maybe." She shrugged again. "But sketching faces won't pay the rent, nor keep Jane and Randy in college, nor Mom in nail polish and manicures."

"Can't you hire a business manager?"

"Not if I'm going to juggle expenses and keep everyone moving forward."

"It's a damn shame," he said bluntly.

"Someday, when Jane's done with med school and Randy has his doctorate, I'll get back to drawing. And painting. And creating." Her voice turned wistful as she stared at the picture of Kari, grinning impishly. Then she visibly drew herself up. "Dad's office is just down here." She walked briskly away.

Trey followed, wondering if he'd ever met a woman as self-sacrificing.

Lori tried to concentrate on her work but it was difficult to ignore Trey's presence. Normally she was alone in the office, although the muted sounds of the restaurant and bar were a constant reminder that busy people weren't far away.

Trey had joined her right after lunch. He sat across the room, long legs stretched out beneath the desk. Fingers tapped a tattoo on the keys or maneuvered the mouse as he clicked from one Web site to the next.

She watched him from beneath a screen of half-lowered lashes. He seemed unaware he was being observed, totally focused on the laptop, a faint frown of concentration drawing lines between his dark brows.

He knew Lori was looking at him. Each time she glanced over, he felt her gaze as if she reached out and stroked her palm over his skin. Much as he wanted to test her interest, he was determined not to respond. He needed access to her computer and was damned if he'd do anything to make her reconsider letting him share her office for the afternoon. He wouldn't have been here at all but the library was closed today.

The door opened suddenly and Risa walked in, destroying the relative quiet and drawing both Trey and Lori's attention.

"I need some cash from the safe, Lori. The Fashion Shoppe is having a sale."

"Can't you write a check?"

"My account is overdrawn again. I gave you my check register yesterday, remember? You said you'd talk to the bank and straighten it out, but in the meantime they tell me I can't use my checkbook."

Trey glanced at Lori and saw her pained resignation before he heard her sigh.

"I'll call them this afternoon. For now, why don't you buy things with your credit card and you can pay it off when your checking account is usable again."

"That won't work."

"Why not?"

"Because I'm over the limit on my card."

Lori drew a deep breath. "You know we can't take money from the business account, Mom."

"I didn't ask you to take it from the account. Just give me a few hundred out of petty cash in the safe."

"I can't do that, either," Lori said patiently.

"Of course you can. Your father used to do it all the time." Risa was visibly upset, her toe tapping a quick rhythm against the wooden floor.

"I'm sure he did, Mom, but things are different now. Each of us draws a monthly income from the trust and all the profit from the business has to be itemized, including petty cash. The books are audited regularly by Dad's estate attorney. We can't take money out unless it's for the restaurant or bar."

"That's ridiculous!" Risa's voice rose. "It's my money."

"Yes, Mom, but now it's mixed with Jane's, Randy's and my money, too, which is controlled by the trust fund and reviewed by someone outside the family." Lori rubbed her forehead. "None of us can help ourselves to money directly from the business."

"I don't know what your father was thinking when he did this," Risa fumed tearfully. "Other husbands leave their estate to their wives."

"Yes," Lori said solemnly. "I know."

"It's outrageous," Risa went on, her hands fluttering in agitation.

"It is," Lori sighed. "Why don't you go shopping, and if you find something you can't live without, maybe Annette can hold it for you until I can visit the bank and straighten out the glitch in your checking account."

"All right. But I'm not happy about the way my money is being handled. I want you to talk to Warren and tell him I expect him to do something. His attorney fees are being paid by the trust, which means he works for us, and he absolutely must find a way to solve this." Risa spun on her stiletto heels and stalked out of the office, dabbing at her eyes with a tissue.

Lori groaned and dropped her head into her hands. "I'm sorry you had to hear that," she said, her voice muffled.

"Your mother's an interesting woman," Trey said, purposely keeping his voice neutral.

Lori lifted her head and looked at him. "Oh, yes. That she is." Her voice held heartfelt agreement. "I have to lock up and go to the bank. I'm sorry to cut your time short on the Internet." She took her purse from a desk drawer. "Did you learn anything new?"

"No, but your server is much faster." He closed the program and turned off the laptop. "Makes the searching easier."

"Oh, good, I'm glad it's helpful." They stepped into the hall and she turned to lock the door behind them. "I have no idea how long it will take to straighten out things at the bank—maybe the rest of the afternoon."

"Then I'll see you tomorrow." Trey watched her walk off down the hall and wondered if Lori's younger brother and sister were as high mainte-nance as her mother.

* * *

Lori spent the next hour and a half at the bank. Risa's personal check register was filled with scribbled entries that were often difficult to decipher. In the end, the banker agreed to waive the bounced check fees and extend a five-hundred-dollar line of credit until the automatic deposit from her trust fund arrived.

Deciding not to go back to work, Lori went home. Risa wasn't there and the house was quiet, blessedly cool and welcoming. In her bedroom upstairs, she dropped the armload of files and her purse on the bed, and toed off her sandals before padding barefoot into the bathroom. She shook a generous amount of foaming bath salts into the tub and while the water was running she stripped off her clothes and left them lying in a pile on the tiled floor.

Clipping her hair up off her neck, she stepped into the scented water, almost groaning as she settled into its soothing warmth.

What a day. Would Risa ever assume responsibility for the details of her life? Not likely, Lori mused, resting her head on the rim of the tub. Her father had coddled and spoiled their mom in so many ways; now she refused to deal with the simple practicalities other people had to face.

And to make matters worse, Troy had heard the entire conversation. It was one thing for Lori to know her mother was financially irresponsible, but quite another for outsiders to be aware of Risa's spendthrift ways.

And somehow, she realized, she regretted even more that it was Troy, specifically, who had had to witness the spectacle.

It's not as if he hasn't had to deal with her at the bar. So why do I wish he hadn't been in the office when Mom came in this afternoon?

It took several moments of mulling over and considering the question before Lori found an answer. Having Troy know Risa was difficult was bad enough, but having him personally observe the lengths she had to go to in order to cope with her mother, was much worse.

Meeting Troy had shaken her conviction that putting her personal life on hold until her family was settled was not only necessary, but practical. Lately she'd found herself wishing she were free of such obligations and entanglements. Much as she loved her family, Troy made her want things she knew she couldn't have, at least not in the foreseeable future. There was no place for a romantic relationship in her life, there simply weren't enough hours in the day to squeeze in a love affair.

Maybe not, but what about a no-strings, hot-sex-only fling?

The thought popped unbidden into her mind.

The possibility was tempting. She'd never done anything so daring. Not that she was a virgin. The boys she'd dated during high school had been good friends but not lovers and her college boyfriend was charming and attentive during the three years they'd been an item. Unfortunately, no guy had ever driven her wild with passion. During their senior year at college, she'd lost her virginity to her boyfriend but it was such a nonevent that afterward, they'd agreed to be friends and parted amicably. Then her dad had died and she'd raced home. Ever since, life had been too busy to contemplate a relationship with anyone. Besides, she'd known all the eligible men in Granger since they were in diapers together. None of them made her want to tear off their clothes, or hers, and fall into bed.

Until Troy. The mysterious gray-eyed stranger made her feel as hot and bothered as the heroines in the romance novels she loved to read. And she wanted to experience with Troy every one of the things romance heroes did with the women in those books.

Especially after that kiss.

She closed her eyes, reliving the hot rush of awareness she'd felt when he'd pulled her close and pressed his lips to hers with a fierce, carnal heat that melted her bones.

She wanted more. But whether she'd ever follow through on her fantasies was still undecided.

She realized the water was growing cold, her skin puckering from being immersed too long. Water sluiced down her body when she stood, wrapping herself in a towel as she stepped out onto the bath mat.

Moments later, dressed in pajama boxers and a white cotton tank top, she raided the refrigerator and settled in for a quiet night.

At 5:00 a.m. the next morning, Lori left the house and walked to the restaurant. Robins and meadowlarks chirped and swooped over the green stretch of lawn in City Park, deftly avoiding being sprayed by the automatic sprinklers as they landed and tugged worms from the wet earth.

She left the park behind and turned onto Granger's Main Street. The business district was empty and quiet without the hum of motors and pedestrians that would fill it later in the morning.

She sang the lyrics to an Elvis Presley song as she entered the restaurant. She couldn't get the tune, or the words, out of her head.

I've got to convince Ralph to change the music on the jukebox. The chef's love of early-fifties rock 'n' roll was one of the things she enjoyed about him. But he's got to stop playing "Don't Be Cruel" for hours on end, she thought, as she pocketed the old-fashioned key and went inside. The shades were drawn on the street-side windows, making the big room dim. She was so familiar with the arrangement of tables and chairs that she didn't need to switch on a light. Instead, she wound her way across the bar, down the short alleyway that held napkins and silverware, and into the kitchen.

She registered the aroma of freshly brewed coffee at the same moment she saw the outline of a man, standing with his back to her, at the far counter.

Her heart stuttered and she stopped abruptly, catching her breath in an audible gasp. Trey looked over his shoulder, his gaze meeting hers.

"Oh." She flattened her palm over her pounding chest. "It's you. You almost gave me a heart attack. I wasn't expecting anyone to be here."

"Sorry." He glanced past her at the empty doorway. "Where's Ralph? I thought he had the early shift this morning."

"He does," she said, setting her purse and files down on the nearest empty countertop. "But he called last night to say he had car trouble in Havre and can't be here until around ten. Marty's sick so I told Ralph I'd come down and open up so the produce and meat trucks can deliver."

"Ah, I see." He nodded, then yawned and scrubbed a hand down his face. "I'm not exactly awake." He gestured at the coffeemaker. "Ralph told me I could use this if I needed to, and I ran out of coffee upstairs."

"Lucky for me," she said. "I haven't had my morning caffeine fix yet."

His smile was endearingly lopsided. Lori couldn't help grinning back. His dark hair was rumpled, an overnight growth of beard stubble shadowed his jaw and his eyes were heavy-lidded and drowsy. He looked as if he'd rolled out of bed, pulled on a pair of Levi's and headed downstairs while still half-asleep. His feet were bare, the muscles of his chest and arms shadowed and highlighted by the faint light coming through the kitchen's solitary window.

Behind him, the coffeemaker buzzed. He took two mugs from the employee shelf and filled them.

Lori cradled the cup he handed her and perched on the tall stool normally reserved for Ralph.

Neither spoke until their mugs were half-empty.

"Isn't it early for you to be up and about?" Lori asked.

"Yeah, way too early." He refilled her cup, then his, and returned to leaning against the counter, his long legs crossed at the ankle. "I had trouble sleeping last night."

Lori frowned. He didn't appear to be ill, in fact, she'd never seen a healthier-looking guy. "Bad dreams?" she guessed, although he didn't seem the type to be bothered by nightmares, either.

"I think so," he said. "Not sure I'd call them nightmares, exactly, but then I can only remember bits and pieces of them."

"Oh." Surprised, Lori eyed him with interest. "What parts do you remember—anything that might give you a clue about the men who attacked you?"

He shook his head, his features somber. "I didn't dream about being hit. In fact, the pieces of the dreams I recalled when I woke up don't make any sense. They don't seem connected, either."

"I'm guessing they weren't pleasant?"

"No. All of them were about funerals."

She shivered. "Well, that's gloomy. Did you recognize any of the people or maybe the churches?"

"Three of them were in the same church, and I was sitting in a front pew. During the first dream, I was a kid and in the next two I was older. In the fourth dream, I was younger and at a cemetery." He frowned. "In the cemetery dream, I was lying on a hillside with someone else, watching a burial going on below us. Come to think of it, the person at the cemetery was beside me in the church those three times, too."

"Do you think your dreams are actual memories of events in your life? Or could they be allegorical?" She looked at him over the rim of her mug, considering what dreaming about funerals might mean beyond reliving an actual event.

"I don't know," he said. "The person I was with in each of the dreams felt real. I think she's someone I know well—a sister, maybe, or a cousin." He shoved his fingers through his hair and raked it back off his forehead, rumpling it further. "It's so damn frustrating."

"You don't remember your family?" She lowered her cup without drinking, staring at him in surprise. "I knew you were missing the few days before the actual robbery. How much time have you lost?"

He went still and stared at her without blinking for a moment, then his expression became distant, and a muscle flexed along his jaw. Lori had the distinct impression he hadn't meant her to know his memory loss involved more than a couple of days.

"I have big gaps of time that are totally blank," he finally said. "I don't remember anything about the robbery except there were two men and one of them hit me with a tire iron. Before that—" he shrugged "—it's dicey. Like I said, big gaps and blank spaces."

"I had no idea." She shook her head in disbelief, appalled. "I can't imagine what you've been going through. Has your memory been returning at all?"

"Not as much or as fast as I'd like. But details are coming slowly, a few more every day."

"Have you considered talking to our sheriff? If he circulated your description and photo beyond Granger, maybe someone would recognize you and get in touch."

"Could be, but I think I'll just wait until Bill and his wife return and I can call them." His expression was grim. "If the sheriff makes this public, there's a chance that whoever dumped me on the road in the first place would find out and come looking for me. If the wrong people find me before my memory returns completely, I might not recognize them."

"True, but working behind the bar is just as risky, isn't it? If the people who robbed you happened to walk into the bar, they'd recognize you instantly, but you might not know them."

"Yes, but since Granger is at least a hundred miles away from the ditch where I woke up, the odds are good that won't happen." He narrowed his eyes, considering. "Unless, of course, the people who dumped me are from Granger."

"But that's not likely, is it?" Lori frowned. "I grew up here and know almost everyone, one way or another. I can't think of a single person likely to commit such a crime."

"I hope you're right. If you are, my chances of being found by the wrong people are slim to none, and hiding in plain sight until I can recover is the best bet."

Chapter Five

Trey left Lori discussing Ralph's order of fresh vegetables with the delivery driver. He went upstairs, where he crawled back into bed. After several hours of sleep, more coffee and a plate of spaghetti, by one in the afternoon he was feeling much more himself.

I shouldn't have told Lori I can't remember my family, he thought as he reentered his apartment after eating in the kitchen downstairs. If she decides to help Troy Jones find his parents or brothers or whoever he's got, I'm in trouble.

And from what he'd observed so far, it would be just like her to care enough to become involved.

He tossed the apartment key on the table and raised the blinds. The window looked out on the alley that ran behind the bar and restaurant. Directly across from him were the wide double doors on the second floor of the local feed store that were used to load and unload hay. Below the hayloft, at alley level, was the rear entrance to the store.

As he stared broodingly down at the empty passage, Lori exited the restaurant and crossed the alley to disappear through the back door of the feed store. Her hair gleamed silver beneath the hot sun, falling in a spill of platinum down her back. She wore a green cotton top, faded blue jeans covered her long legs and she carried a sheaf of papers in one hand.

On impulse and with a vague idea that he should find a way to convince her not to get involved in his identity search, Trey left the apartment, jogging down the back stairs to the alleyway.

Lori waved a hello at the clerk behind the feed store counter. Busy with a customer, he lifted a hand in acknowledgment and she climbed the wood plank stairs to the second floor.

Ashworths had rented storage space here since her grandfather's day, and as a child she'd often come here with her father and played in the hay while he inventoried supplies in their section.

The dozen keys on the large brass ring jingled and jangled as she searched and finally found the large one that fit the old lock.

Outside, the hot sunshine dimmed and thunder rumbled in the distance.

I hope it rains. The early-morning weather report had predicted thunderstorms and lightning but whether it would also bring rain was questionable. She hoped so; she loved storms, and her garden and lawn could use the water.

She left the storage room door wide-open to let in the sound of the approaching storm, flicked on the overhead light and, list in hand, started down the first aisle. She worked her way halfway down the row of shelves, counting the number of napkins and making a note to order more.

"Hey."

Startled, she looked over her shoulder. Trey strolled toward her.

"Hi." She smiled, delighted. "I thought you'd sleep all afternoon since you were up so early this morning."

"I went back to bed after I left the kitchen," he said. "But I seem to be programmed to wake up around noon."

"I think most people who work the late shift are. Off work at 2:00 a.m., bed by three or four, and up again at noon. Crazy hours for some folks. Does it bother you?"

"Doesn't seem to."

"Maybe you're naturally wired to be a night person."

"Could be." He looked at the documents in her hand, then glanced at the shelves. "What are you doing?"

"Checking inventory." She rolled her eyes and made a face. "One of my least favorite chores."

"Want some help?"

"I'd love some. Are you sure you want to spend your afternoon counting cocktail napkins and stir sticks?"

"Absolutely."

She laughed. "Okay, but just remember when you get bored, you volunteered. It's not my fault."

"I won't blame you." He gestured toward the papers she held. "Do you want to take notes while I count?"

"Sure, that would be great."

"Wait a second." He disappeared through the doorway and came back carrying a short wooden stepladder. "Here, you can sit on this."

"Thank you." *Not only is he gorgeous, he's thoughtful. I wonder how I can convince him to stay in Granger permanently?*

Time passed as they moved up and down the aisles, talking while they worked. They discovered they didn't always agree—he was a Republican, she leaned toward the Democratic party. They both loved country and western music and classic rock 'n' roll, agreeing they'd grown more fond of Elvis since working with Ralph.

Lori wanted to ask him if there were areas of his life in which he could remember his favorite things, like music, and areas he couldn't. But she didn't want to destroy the easy camaraderie between them, so she contented herself with letting the conversation drift where it would.

"That's all of it," she said as she jotted down a total for reams of computer paper stored on the last shelf. She slipped off her perch on the ladder and turned to fold it.

"I'll get that." Trey reached past her, his arm brushing hers, and picked up the stepladder.

"Thanks." Her skin heated where he touched her, awareness sizzling along her nerve endings.

As they reentered the part of the loft used to store hay, thunder roared and boomed, filling the open space with noise.

Startled, Lori jumped and dropped the sheaf of papers. "Shoot," she muttered, bending to retrieve them.

Trey leaned the ladder against the wall and went down on one knee to help gather the scattered sheets.

The double doors looking out on the alley stood open, but instead of the bright sunshine that had poured in when they'd started the inventory, the sky outside now rolled with black clouds. The far corners of the room were shadowy, the rafters beneath the roof lost in gloom.

Just as they collected the last of the spilled documents and Trey stood, the skies opened and rain bucketed down. It pounded on the roof and quickly sluiced in rivers from the eaves, bouncing on the pavement below.

Lori crossed to the doors and peered out, taking care to keep far enough back to avoid the splashes that spattered the rough wood floor in front of the wide opening. "I love storms, don't you?" She turned her face up, drawing in the moist scent, mixed with the pungent aroma of dried alfalfa in the loft.

"Yeah, I do." He joined her, standing just behind her, not quite touching. "I guess we aren't going anywhere, not unless you're willing to get soaking wet."

She looked down at the alley, where water ran in rivulets. "We'd be drenched, even though it wouldn't take more than a few seconds to get to the bar. It's pouring out there."

For several moments they stood quietly, watching the rain, whipped by occasional gusts of wind, come down in sheets and then settle into a steady downpour.

"It looks like we're going to be here awhile." Trey left her and took a bright red wool blanket from atop a saddle on a nearby sawhorse. "Might as well get comfortable."

He shook out the throw, letting it settle over a pile of loose hay and looked at her, his expression enigmatic.

Lori hesitated, and a slow smile curved his mouth.

"I don't bite," he drawled. "At least, not unless you want me to."

"Then I don't have anything to worry about, do I?" she replied, mimicking his drawl.

He laughed, his eyes lighting with amusement, and she stepped past him to sink onto the blanket. The hay beneath made a comfortable cushion and she slipped off her sandals, put her papers and pen on the floor, then drew up her knees and wrapped her arms around them. She rested her chin on her knees, staring out the doors at the falling rain.

Trey's weight rustled the hay as he settled beside her. "After all the hot days, it's nice to smell rain."

She nodded. "It feels like we're cut off from the world, doesn't it? In a way, I suppose we are. No one's likely to venture out in the wet."

The deluge outside created a cocoon of privacy, intimate and quiet.

"I used to come up here with my dad when I was a little girl," Lori commented.

"Did you help him take inventory?"

Lori shook her head. "Not until I was older. When I was really little, maybe three or four, I played in the hay." She laid her palm flat on the blanket. "Sometimes I'd climb into one of the saddles stored up here and pretend I was a cowgirl."

Trey's hand covered hers. "You miss him, don't you?"

"Yes." She glanced at him and he seemed suddenly closer, looming over her. "Troy…"

"Yeah?" His voice was lower, rougher.

"I don't make a habit of grabbing strange men at ball games and kissing them. Especially when they work for me. In some circles, that's called sexual harassment. In fact," she added over his instant laugh, "I can't think of one single prior instance when I've done that. Just in case you were thinking that was normal for me—I wanted to make it clear, it's not."

"Here's what I think…" His hand closed over the curve of her shoulder, his gray eyes dark as the storm outside. "I think the kiss in the bleachers ended way too soon. I think we should try it again—so I can find out if you taste as good as I remember."

"You do?" she murmured, her voice a husky thread of sound.

"Yeah." He bent toward her, his lips brushing hers. "I do," he whispered. And with slow precision, he fit his mouth over hers.

The same hot flush of need and yearning that she'd felt at the ball game washed over her. She felt wooed, drugged by the seductive movement of his warm lips.

He pushed her gently down on the blanket, following to half-lie over her, his kisses turning urgent.

"Hey, Lori, you up there?"

The male voice startled them. Lori froze and Trey lifted his head, his eyes heavy and slumberous.

"You've got a phone call—it's Ralph. Says he needs to talk to you."

"I'll be right down, Jess." To her surprise, her voice sounded almost normal.

Trey rolled to his feet and held out his hand. She let him pull her to her feet, brushing stray bits of hay from her hair.

"We'll continue this later?" he murmured, his gaze following the movements of her hands.

"Yes, let's."

His eyes gleamed and he smiled, standing back to let her walk ahead of him down the stairs.

Much to Lori's delight, over the next few days Trey made a habit of stopping by her office mid-morning to say hello before joining Ralph in the kitchen. The two men seemed to have bonded over food prep and chopping knives, a fact which made her smile since she adored Ralph and was becoming increasingly charmed by Trey.

She knew he would be leaving in a few weeks and returning to Four Buttes, but in the meantime she saw no harm in flirting with him. Whether or not she wanted more than hot kisses was still undecided.

One evening, she stayed late in the office, struggling to locate an accounting glitch that had her baffled.

Lori frowned at the screen. *Why isn't this balancing?* According to the register receipts, she was short twenty dollars from last night's cash.

It took a half hour to pinpoint the problem. She saved the data to a disk and filed it away, then shut off her computer.

"Hey."

Trey leaned against the doorjamb, his arms crossed.

"Hello." She couldn't help but smile. Just seeing him made her heart sing. *No guy should look this good.* He wore jeans, boots and a black T-shirt with the logo Granger Bar in small white type on the left side.

"You're working late tonight."

"I know." She waved a hand at the pile of register tape, sales slips and the money bag atop her desk. "It took me forever to find a twenty-dollar shortage. Turns out one of the waitresses punched in forty-three instead of twenty-three when she rang out a customer."

"Easy enough to do. Are you almost finished?" he asked, one dark eyebrow arching upward.

"I just turned off my computer," she said with satisfaction.

"I'm not working tonight. How about having dinner with me before you go home?"

She glanced at the clock. It was six-thirty. "I hadn't realized how late it was." She pressed a hand to her midriff. "Nor how hungry I am. I'd love to join you."

He waited while she cleared her desk, slipped the cash and checks along with the receipts into a bank bag before tucking it into the wall safe.

"Do you want to eat here?" she asked.

"If you'd like to—or is there someplace else in town you'd rather go?"

"I love the Italian food at Uncle Joe's," she confessed. "Do you like pizza?"

"Love it," he said emphatically.

"Great, it's just down the block."

The restaurant was redolent with the aroma of Italian cooking. Trey's eyes half-closed. "Tell me that's lasagna I small." His voice was reverent.

Lori grinned. "Actually, it's the best lasagna in Montana."

"Yeah?" He eyed her with interest. "How do you know?"

"Because Joe says so." She took his arm and drew him toward an empty booth. "He's Italian and swears his lasagna is truly the best in Montana."

They lingered over pizza and lasagna, accompanied by glasses of the house wine, before Trey walked her home in the warm darkness.

It wasn't until he'd kissed her good-night and she was lying in bed that she realized he'd asked her lots of questions about her life in Granger, but had shared little about himself.

Her smile turned to a faint frown.

Was he being purposely enigmatic? Or was he simply interested in her?

Tomorrow I'm going to make him tell me what he does with his free time when he's in Four Buttes. She punched her pillow and rolled over, her frown deepening. She'd never met a guy who didn't want to talk about himself. Curiouser and curiouser, she thought drowsily.

Chapter Six

"Are you sure you want to go out with Harry again?" Lori dropped a cherry into a glass of vanilla-flavored cola and set it on the bar in front of her mother. "This is your sixth date. He might think you're serious."

"Don't you like Harry?" Risa asked, carefully pulling the glass nearer with her fingertips. She sipped, then put it back down on the counter to frown at her fresh, not-quite-dry red nail polish. "I'm not sure about this color—does it really match my lipstick?"

Lori glanced from the long, scarlet fingernails with their tiny starburst pattern to Risa's pursed lips. "Yes, definitely."

"Good." Risa hummed with satisfaction and smoothed her palm over the red-poppies-on-white-background silk skirt. "I hoped it would, but didn't have my dress or the lipstick with me when I picked it out."

Her mother's attention still on her nails, Lori rolled her eyes in exasperation. She had a healthy interest in fashion, but her mother's endless fascination with the details of her appearance often made Lori want to tear her hair and groan with frustration. Besides, Risa often used her obsession with fashion trivia to avoid questions she didn't want to answer, like the current one about Harry.

"Does Harry like scarlet?" Lori asked.

Risa flicked her a swift accusatory glance. "I don't know."

"Hmm." Lori hid a smile.

"Why are you working behind the bar?" Risa swept the room with a searching gaze. "Where's Troy?"

"He went to get a case of ginger ale from the storeroom in the kitchen. Did you need him for something?"

"No, I just wondered where he was. It seems I rarely see one of you without the other lately."

Lori busied herself washing the few dirty glasses, avoiding her mother's sharp eyes. "He's been very helpful and given me some good ideas for streamlining service and making the business run more efficiently."

"And how come he knows so much about managing a restaurant and bar?" Risa asked. "He seems way more experienced than an ordinary bartender."

"I suppose because he's worked in a lot of different places," Lori replied. "And he's intelligent, with an interest in the industry—I assume he gained expertise with each new job."

"Humph," Risa sniffed. "Maybe. But if you ask me, there's something not quite right about your Mr. Jones."

"He's not my Mr. Jones," Lori said.

"Well he certainly acts like it. He's hardly looked at another woman since he started working here. And don't think they haven't been flirting with him."

"I'm sure they have. He's a very attractive man, Mom," Lori said reasonably, hiding the burst of pleasure at her mother's observation that Troy wasn't interested in anyone else. She picked up a towel and began to dry the clean glasses.

A man and woman entered, pausing to look around the bar, empty at the moment except for Lori and Risa.

"Good morning," Lori called, glad for the interruption. She really didn't want to discuss Troy with her mother, especially since she couldn't figure out exactly where her relationship with him stood. "Come in and have a seat," she invited.

They weren't locals. The man was tall with a powerful build and an air of authority. He had black hair and a strong-boned, handsome face with ice-blue eyes beneath the brim of his white Stetson. Despite the hat, boots and jeans, he didn't look like an ordinary rancher, Lori thought.

The woman clung to his hand, her face pale and tense beneath her thick mahogany mane.

"What can I get you?" Lori asked as they took seats at the bar, separated from Risa by two blue-covered stools. There was something oddly familiar about the woman, but Lori couldn't put her finger on it. But she was sure she hadn't met her or her companion before.

"Just coffee," the big man said.

Lori took two mugs from the shelf behind her, her back to the room as she reached for the coffeepot.

"And a little information," he added.

"What kind of information?" Lori filled the two mugs and turned to set them atop cocktail napkins on the bar in front of the couple.

"We're looking for this man." He slid a photo across the counter toward her. "Have you seen him?"

Risa's glass hit the bar with a decided clink and she leaned forward to peer at the picture.

Lori stared at the photo of Troy. He looked younger, caught smiling at the camera, and his right temple was smooth and unblemished, with no sign of a scar.

"Yes." She tore her attention from Troy's image and looked at the man. "I have."

The woman at his side gasped. "When? Where?"

Before Lori could reply, a loud crash shattered the tension.

"Damn." Trey's voice preceded him into the room. All four turned to the hallway door to watch him enter. "Sorry, Lori," he said ruefully. "I knocked over the recycling box again."

"Trey." The dark-haired woman swayed and caught her companion's arm for support.

Troy froze in place, his face expressionless as he met her gaze.

"You're the woman in my dreams," he said slowly.

A sense of betrayal sent a swift stab of pain through Lori's chest. "You dream about her?" She stared at the woman. Once again she was struck by the familiar features. Tears glistened in eyes that were thick-lashed and dark gray…

Lori caught her breath as she looked from the woman to Trey and back again. "You two are so much alike—the same eyes…"

"We're twins." The brunette swiped tears from her cheeks with her fingertips, her voice trembling, those gray eyes fastened on Trey. "We've been searching for you."

"Have you? I wondered if I'd been missed somewhere." He set the box down on the closest table.

He joined Lori behind the bar, only a few feet from the stool where the woman sat, tense and clearly emotional. She groaned. "You've been hurt. What happened?"

"Well, that's the strange thing." He brushed his fingers over the scar on his temple. "I don't know."

"You don't know?" the tall cattleman said, his voice mild. "Or you don't remember?"

"Same thing."

"Not always."

"You don't remember, do you?" Anxiety etched the brunette's face. "Do you know who I am, Trey?"

Trey? Lori felt her eyes widen in disbelief. She abruptly realized the woman had called him Trey twice now. But his name was Troy—wasn't it?

"Do you know who *you* are?" the man asked.

"That's a loaded question," Trey answered. "Few people know who they really are."

"You don't know." The brunette frowned, clearly confused. "No matter." She shook her head. "Your name is Trey Harper and you're my brother. Did you receive a blow to the head when you got the scar? If so, you could have amnesia." She leaned closer. "Look at me—really look at me. We're twins. We have the same color eyes, the same bone structure."

"Seems obvious to me," Risa interrupted. "The two of you are as alike as peas in a pod. Except one of you is male and the other female." She leaned forward to whisper. "I think it's safe to tell your sister what you know."

"Mother..." Lori protested, wishing Risa wouldn't get involved. One thing was glaringly clear. The man she'd known as Troy Jones was someone else entirely. *He lied to me.* Anger was quickly replacing stunned shock and disbelief.

"It's all right, Lori," he said.

No, it's not. Rage surged through her before she belatedly realized Troy…no, *Trey,* was referring to her mother's comments, not to his lying.

"I don't see any harm in telling my sister…" Trey continued before he broke off to stare intently at the brunette. "I remember your face, but not your name."

"It's Raine. And this is Chase McCloud."

Lori went still. Chase McCloud? No wonder the man exuded power. His family was one of the richest in the state of Montana. Was Troy—*Trey,* she corrected—was Trey connected to the McClouds?

"This is Lori Ashworth and her mother, Risa," Trey said after he and Chase shook hands. "They own this bar and the restaurant next door."

Risa tapped her long red fingernails on the counter and assessed the couple. "Chase McCloud? Even in our little town we've heard of the McCloud family and Wolf Creek. I admit, when our boy, here—" she pointed at Trey "—walked in a few weeks ago and told us he didn't remember a thing, I doubted whether it was true. I even wondered if he was running a scam of some sort. But now that you've identified him, well…it's not likely he would have voluntarily left Wolf Creek to work for us in little old Granger, now, is it?" She smiled. "Is there a reward for keeping him safe?"

"Mother!" Lori groaned. Trey squeezed her shoulder, and she shifted away from his touch, unable to bear his hand on her skin. The sense of betrayal grew stronger by the second.

"I hadn't thought about a reward," Raine said, looking at Trey as if for guidance. "I believe I'll leave that up to my brother, since only he knows how safe he's been."

"We'll talk about it later," Trey said, his voice even.

Risa shrugged. "Can't blame a woman for trying." She gestured at Raine. "I think you should tell her what you told us happened to you."

"Yes," Raine agreed quickly. "Please do."

The outside door opened and two cowboys entered to take seats a few feet beyond Risa.

"Why don't you move to a table so you can talk without being overheard," Lori managed to say quietly. "I'll deal with the customers."

"Join us," Trey said. "Jeannie can take over for a few minutes."

She hesitated, torn between her anger and a need to hear the reasoning behind his charade.

Trey leaned past her to push the call button next to the cash register. "I can sense the wheels turning inside your head. Don't convict me until you've heard all the facts," he said grimly.

She stared at him for a long silent moment. He didn't look away, and her gaze didn't shift from his. "I'll take the cowboys' order while we're waiting for Jeannie," she said finally.

By the time the group had moved to a table in the corner, Jeannie arrived to mind the bar and Lori joined them. She took a seat beside Risa, purposely leaving the chair next to Trey empty.

"Please," Raine was saying as Lori sat down, "tell us what happened."

"There's not much to tell," Trey began. "I woke up along the highway one morning a few weeks ago. There was a lump and a cut on my head and I couldn't remember my name or where I lived. A trucker gave me as ride a far as Granger, and I walked in here where Lori and Risa took pity on me. They cleaned me up, let me use a vacant apartment upstairs, and gave me a job."

Lori thought, you've conveniently left out the

part where you let us believe you were someone else—someone we trusted.

"Did you see a doctor?" Raine asked.

"Yeah. He stitched me up, gave me some painkillers and told me not to worry about my memory—said in his experience, most cases like mine resolved themselves within a few weeks."

"And has it? Begun to resolve itself, I mean." Raine studied his face intently.

"I remember bits and pieces. Like tending bar and a killer recipe for nachos."

His sister's eyes brightened and she laughed. "With jalapeños?"

"So hot it burns all the way down," Trey agreed, grinning.

"It's one of your specialties at home," she murmured, smiling at him.

"So," Chase commented. "The doctor was right. You're starting to remember."

"Apparently."

The first of the regular after-work crowd came in. They'd barely filled the chairs at one table when another group surged through the entrance, chattering and laughing. Behind the bar, Jeannie gestured frantically at Lori.

She shoved back her chair and stood. "It was

lovely meeting you, Raine—and Chase—but I'm afraid I have to get back to work."

"Me, too," Trey said. "Are you staying in Granger tonight?" he asked Raine.

"Yes."

"Good, I don't finish until midnight. Maybe we can get together for breakfast tomorrow?"

"Of course."

"Can you recommend a local motel?" Chase asked.

"Granger only has one—Reed's Inn, on the outskirts of town near the highway exit," Lori replied.

"Thanks." Chase touched the brim of his hat and took Raine's arm.

Lori watched the couple walk away, still stunned by their revelations, her temper simmering. "It's going to take a while to get used to calling you Trey." Her words carried a sarcastic bite.

"Yeah." He continued staring at the empty doorway where Raine and Chase had disappeared. "After all the mystery, it seems a little surreal to finally know the truth."

She narrowed her eyes. "I don't suppose you have any idea what happened to the real Troy Jones?"

"No." He met her gaze without flinching. "I know I owe you an apology," he said abruptly.

"Yes, you do." At the very least, she thought, purposely drawing several deep breaths in an attempt to defuse her fury. "But a crowded bar isn't the place to have that conversation. Do you remember everything now?"

"No." He shook his head. "Bits and pieces, flashes of scenes." He grimaced. "To be honest, it's giving me a hell of a headache."

She fought down instinctive concern. Damn him. Why should she care if he was suffering? "Should I call in Butch to cover your shift?"

"No," he said decisively. "I've had worse headaches. I'm hoping they'll be gone for good once my memory returns completely." He glanced at the now-crowded room. "Before you joined us at the table, Raine told me she and I own several businesses in Wolf Creek, including one called the Saloon. It's a western place with an attached restaurant."

"Which explains why you know how to tend bar," Lori said. "And I thought it was because you've been working for Bill for the last three years."

The place had been almost empty all night. With Jeannie's urging, Trey left the Granger Bar shortly after ten-thirty, the night air warm on his bare arms. Lori had treated him with icy reserve until she'd left for home around nine o'clock. He didn't know how the hell to explain and he was damned if he'd try with a bar full of people hearing everything.

With a few simple words, his sister had handed him his identity and given him back his life. Those same few words had cost him Lori's trust.

Bad luck. Bad timing, he thought. He'd known, by the flush of anger in her cheeks, the instant she realized he'd lied to her. The hot glitter of her eyes had become frosted green glass by the time she left the bar.

Only a cool sliver of moon hung high in the black, star-spangled sky and the streets were quiet, the sound of the jukebox growing muted and finally fading away altogether. He was two blocks away from the bar and crossing the opening of an alleyway when the back of his neck tingled in warning. Instinct told him he wasn't alone on the empty street. He glanced down the gap between the buildings but it was a dark tunnel where nothing moved.

He walked faster, scanning the sidewalk ahead and behind. He found nothing to confirm his gut feeling that he was being watched. Nevertheless, the conviction didn't go away. He stopped with his back to the brick wall of the Granger Pharmacy and slipped the knife from his boot, palming it.

He left the business section behind and reached the residential area, lit by streetlights and the golden glow that spilled onto lawns from the open doors and windows of the houses. Here the shadows were darker beneath overhanging branches of leafy trees.

At the end of the last block of homes and a short half mile from the highway was Reed's Inn. The small, neatly kept motel had twelve units and boasted a swimming pool in a chain-link enclosure. Climbing roses spilled over one end of the fence, throwing puddles of shade over the concrete pad surrounding the pool.

Dusty pickup trucks were parked in front of four of the units, and an expensive-looking black SUV sat outside a fifth. Trey took a chance and knocked on the door. Almost immediately it opened and Chase waved him inside. Trey stepped over the threshold, glancing over his shoulder.

"I might have been followed." He frowned. Had he imagined the feeling he was being watched?

"Why would someone be following you?" Chase asked, giving the night a swift, sweeping scan before closing the door and locking it.

"I don't know." He glanced at Raine, who was curled up on pillows propped against the bed's headboard. The remote control for the television lay beside her and she was dressed in a light tank top and pajama bottoms while Chase wore only a pair of Levi's. A huge black rottweiler sprawled on the floor by the bed. He opened one eye to stare at Trey, then woofed softly and went back to sleep.

Chase didn't question him further, instead he nodded at the dining area in the corner of the room. "Have a seat."

Raine left the bed and joined them, tucking one leg beneath her to perch on a chair. "You ordered those boots from a shop in Dallas." She pointed at his feet. "They were custom-made and the boot-maker stamped your initials, TH, in the tool work just above the ankle on the inside of each boot."

Taken aback at the ease with which she explained one of the many things he'd wondered about over the last weeks, Trey raked his hand through his hair. "Damn. You're right." He pulled out a chair and straddled it, his forearms resting on the back. "After you left the bar, I borrowed Lori's office computer and ran a search on your name. You're listed as the owner of a business in Wolf Creek, together with a brother named Trey."

"But you still don't remember Raine or your life in Wolf Creek?" Chase asked.

"I've been having flashes, bits and pieces of memories, but I don't have a full picture yet."

"Maybe it would be easier if you told us what you *do* remember," Chase suggested.

"I have no clear memory of a life prior to roughly three or four weeks ago when I woke up in a ditch…"

An hour later Trey left the motel room. Talking with his sister and Chase had given him a lot of information and explained a great deal, but left several major questions unanswered.

For him, the world had shifted on its axis, but Granger seemed oblivious. The moon was still a sliver of pale white, the residential streets quiet. The houses that had been well lit earlier were now dark as neighborhoods slept.

Trey moved quickly down the sidewalk. The sixth sense that had warned him of danger earlier was calm, and he reached Lori's house without incident. The drapes were drawn and no lamplight glowed behind the blank windows.

He debated walking away without disturbing her. But if he did, he might have to leave town before talking to her.

"Oh, what the hell," he muttered and jabbed the button for the doorbell. She was already furious with him—how much madder could she get if he woke her?

Seconds ticked by and he was about to push the bell again when a light switched on inside and the door opened abruptly. Lori looked at him through the screen. Her hair hung in a thick sheaf of silver down her back and she wore a short blue cotton robe, her thighs bare beneath the short hem.

"What are you doing here?" she demanded.

"I need to talk to you."

"It's the middle of the night. Can't it wait until tomorrow?"

"No, it can't."

"Why not?"

"Because I'm leaving town in the morning," he said flatly.

She stared at him for a moment, then silently pushed the screen door open.

He brushed past her into the entryway, and the clean scent of her floral shampoo reached his nostrils. The smell instantly roused memories he couldn't forget—Lori cheering with excitement at the ball field just before she grabbed and kissed him—Lori in the hayloft with her hair spread beneath her, white-blond against the red blanket. A dozen more snapshots flickered through his mind, swift as lightning, and the knowledge that he had to leave her tomorrow hit him like a blow.

He caught the edge of the door in one hand and pushed it shut as he wrapped his other arm around her and backed her against the closed door.

She sputtered and slapped her palms against his chest, shoving hard.

He bent his head and covered her mouth with his but she stiffened with rejection, her lips stubbornly closed.

Just when he realized he should let her go, she melted and reached for him, her arms circling his neck, her hands closing into fists in his hair. Her lips parted and she kissed him back, her mouth hot and fiercely passionate.

He fought down the urge to pick her up and carry her to bed. She deserved the truth, at least as much of it as he knew.

On the other hand, if he gave her time to think, she'd probably kick him out.

Helluva choice, he thought, and reluctantly broke free.

"We need to talk." He gently held her wrists and pressed a kiss into her palms.

"Let go of me." She jerked away from him, her voice husky with the remnants of passion and returning anger. "And get out of my house."

"Give me ten minutes—just ten minutes," he repeated as she opened her mouth. "If you still want to throw me out after I tell you what little I know, then I'll leave."

She glared at him for a long moment, her curiosity seeming to battle with her desire to want him gone.

"All right," she said at last. "Come into the living room." She pulled the loosened edges of her light cotton robe together and snugged the belt tighter, then walked away from him.

He sighed with relief and followed her. She pointedly walked past the sofa and sat in an overstuffed chair, tucking her feet beneath her.

Trey glanced at the nearest seat, several feet away, and opted to perch on the end of the heavy coffee table, which brought him inches away from her bare toes.

She drew her feet closer and frowned at him.

He leaned forward, propping his elbows on his thighs and met her gaze. "I never meant to lie to you." He ignored her sniff of disbelief and kept talking. "When I woke up in that ditch, I couldn't remember my name or where I came from. The only clue I had was the Granger postmark on a letter I found nearby. That's why I hitched a ride here. I had hardly any money, and all I knew was two men had hit me with a tire iron. When you called me Troy Jones and seemed to realize who I was, I went along with it. Hell, for all I knew, maybe I really *was* Jones."

"If you thought you might be, then why didn't you call the sheriff in Four Buttes and find out more information? The real Troy Jones has worked there for several years. There must have been someone in town who could have identified you." She crossed her arms and glared at him. "If I'd had any sense, that's what I should have done instead of accepting what you told me."

"I couldn't contact the sheriff."

"Why not?" Disbelief rang in her voice.

"Because while I wanted to learn my identity, I also knew someone had tried to kill me. You and Kari didn't recognize me and you've lived in Granger all your lives, which convinced me it wasn't likely I'd ever spent any time here. It also meant that whoever threw me in that ditch wouldn't come looking for me in Granger. It was a safe place for me to hide while I waited for my memory to return."

"But it didn't return."

"No, not completely. And not bringing the details I most wanted—my name and where I'm from. Not until my sister tracked me down. I learned quite a bit from Raine and Chase tonight. They've been hunting for me nonstop since I disappeared. The last time my sister saw me, I was planning a trip down to Billings, driving south from my home in Wolf Creek. That's where they concentrated their search, but Granger is more than a hundred miles north and east of Wolf Creek, which meant they were looking in the wrong direction."

"What made them come to Granger?" Her voice held reluctant curiosity.

"The authorities found my SUV abandoned south of here. Chase identified the red clay mud on the wheels and knew it was common in this area."

"Do they know who attacked you and why?"

"No." He looked at her, wishing he could get past her rage. "I came to Granger because of the postmark on that envelope I found in the ditch. It held a letter that was sent to my home, asking me to meet the anonymous writer at a bar in Billings. My sister says I left Wolf Creek to keep the appointment and that was the last they heard of me, until today." He ran his hand through his hair. "That's why I'm going with them to Wolf Creek tomorrow. I need to know what happened, and my best chance of finding out is to go back to where it started."

"That makes sense," she said evenly. "And your home is there. It's where you belong." She rose abruptly and moved away from him. "If you'll send me your address in Wolf Creek, I'll forward your paycheck. You can leave your keys to the apartment and the restaurant with Butch in the morning."

"Lori…" He stood, but when he walked toward her, she stepped behind a chair, effectively using its bulk as a barrier between them. "I didn't want to lie to you. You have to believe me."

"It doesn't matter, Troy—Trey." She crossed her arms over her midriff, her gaze holding his. "It's good we both learned the truth now, before either of us became emotionally attached to the other. This way nobody gets hurt. No harm, no foul, right?"

Was she kidding? He stared at her but she didn't blink or look away. At last he shrugged. "Yeah, right." He pulled the door open, pausing once more to look back at her. "I'll be in touch."

She didn't move or reply. He left, feeling as if

he'd been sucker punched, her rejection burning a hole in his chest.

Lori stayed behind the chair, holding herself rigidly erect until the screen door slammed shut and the sound of his footsteps faded into silence. Then she moved, mechanically resetting the dead bolt on the door before she turned and climbed the stairs.

She felt numb, her movements automatic as she shed her robe, letting it drop on the carpet and climbed back into her bed to stare unseeingly at the ceiling.

He's leaving. It's over. I'll never see him again.

Her hard-won composure collapsed, a flood of emotion and feelings washing over her and she curled on her side, tears streaming down her face.

Chapter Seven

Trey tossed and turned, unable to sleep.

I should have found a way to tell her the truth earlier.

He knew he'd put off explaining because he'd been afraid Lori would react just as she had. He'd wanted to delay the day when she inevitably learned he'd lied to her and she threw him out of her life.

I'm not giving up, he thought. I have to go back to Wolf Creek tomorrow but as soon as I get answers to who I am and what happened, I'm coming back. If I have to, I'll camp on her doorstep until she lets me in and listens to me.

Just after 5:30 a.m., he heard Ralph downstairs. He abandoned any hope of sleeping and within a half hour he was downstairs with a small duffel bag full of the few belongings he'd collected during the weeks he'd been in Granger.

The cook stood in front of the coffeemaker across the kitchen, his back to the doorway, when Trey appeared.

"'Morning, Ralph." He hesitated, not willing to enter until he was invited.

The stocky chef glanced over his shoulder, his gaze flicking over the duffel bag, before he turned back to the counter. "Come in. Coffee's done."

Evidently Ralph hadn't passed judgment yet, Trey thought, as he took a seat at the end of the island.

Ralph set one of the full mugs of coffee he carried in front of Trey and sat on the stool across from him. Neither spoke as they drank and several moments passed in silence.

"I understand you had a visit from your sister yesterday," Ralph said at last.

"Yeah."

"And that you aren't Troy Jones after all, is that right?"

Trey nodded.

"You want to explain how that happened?" Ralph said mildly.

Trey told him as much as he knew. When he finished, Ralph contemplated him, then quietly refilled their cups.

"You remember what I told you, the first day we met—about how we think a lot of Lori?" He paused and Trey nodded. "Maybe you'd like to tell me why I shouldn't throw you out on the street for hurting my girl."

If anyone else but Ralph had asked him, Trey would have refused to comment, but he knew Ralph had assumed the role of protector after Lori's father died.

"Because I'm going to marry her—if she'll have me," he said bluntly.

Ralph visibly relaxed. "What makes you think she will?" he asked. "Seems to me you've got one hell of a lot of fast talking to do if you're going to convince her you're worth her time."

"Don't I know it," Trey muttered, half to himself.

Ralph lifted his cup in salute. "Here's wishing

you luck, boy. It should be entertaining watching you try, if nothing else."

Chase and Raine pulled up in front of the bar at exactly ten, and Trey was waiting on the sidewalk.

He tossed his bag ahead of him onto the floor of the SUV, slid into the back seat after it, and came face-to-face with the huge rottweiler.

"Whoa." He froze. The dog didn't wag his tail, but he didn't growl, either. He stared steadily at Trey, his mouth open as he panted.

"Killer, behave yourself," Chase said mildly.

"Does he bite?" Trey asked, cautiously closing the door and fastening his seat belt.

"Not unless I tell him to."

"Good. Don't."

Chase chuckled. "I won't."

"Killer's a sweetheart," Raine put in. "He won't bother you."

The rottweiler uttered a low woof and lay down, resting his chin on Trey's thigh.

"I forgot to warn you," Raine said over her shoulder. "He likes to cuddle."

"Cuddle?" Trey said skeptically. "Should I expect him to climb into my lap next?"

"Not unless you let him."

Trey stroked his palm over the dog's head, and he rumbled in appreciation.

"It's like sharing a seat with a bear," he commented. "A friendly bear," he added when Killer licked his hand.

Conversation lapsed. Chase turned on the CD player and a classic rock concert began; Rod Stewart following the Rolling Stones before Bob Seger's voice filled the SUV. Trey closed his eyes and catnapped as the miles rolled by.

When they reached Wolf Creek, however, all traces of drowsiness vanished and he studied the streets intently. To his relief he felt a strong sense of homecoming.

Chase and Raine accompanied him up the back stairs of the saloon to his apartment.

Raine pressed a key into his palm. "You can use mine until you have a duplicate made."

"Thanks." He opened the door, pocketing the key, and went inside. Dropping his duffel on the sofa, he turned in a slow circle. The openness of the apartment gave it a feeling of spaciousness that was magnified by the high ceilings and polished wood floors. The kitchen took up one corner, separated from the big room by a counter where four leather and metal stools were pushed neatly into place beneath the tiled rim. Above the stove, copper-bottomed pans hung from a wrought-iron rack.

An archway on the far side of the room led to a hall; he knew without exploring that the bedroom and bath were located there.

"Does it seem familiar?" Raine asked.

"You know it does." He stared at the kitchen with the gleaming pots, further evidence of his interest in cooking. "I like it," he said. "Feels like a place I might call home."

"Maybe your memory will return faster now that you're here, among friends and your own things." Raine's voice held hope mixed with concern.

"It can't be too soon for me. I'm damned tired of surprises." He meant every word.

"Maybe we should let you settle in by yourself," Chase said.

Raine agreed. "I'll see you later this afternoon, Trey?"

"Sure." He returned her hug, feeling more comfortable with her open affection than he'd been the day before.

"I need a few minutes to talk to Trey, Raine."

Despite Chase's calm manner, the tone of his voice warned Trey something was wrong. His eyes narrowed, trying to work out what it was about the man that had set off his radar as Chase walked Raine out onto the landing.

Trey crossed his arms and leaned against the countertop dividing the kitchen from the living room, waiting.

A moment later Chase reentered and joined him at the counter, his expression forbidding.

"The Sheriff's Office ID'ed Carl and Bobby Rimes from the fingerprints in your vehicle. They've both disappeared and the sheriff believes they know they're wanted for questioning. I need your help to keep Raine safe while I track them down and bring them in."

"You've got it." At last he had names. But he wanted more details. "I don't remember the two— who are they?"

"Carl and Bobby are local brothers in their midthirties. They've been in and out of jail on minor crime convictions since they were teenagers. They've been working as hired hands at Harlan Kerrigan's ranch for the last ten months."

"Kerrigan?" He frowned, trying to recall. "That name's familiar."

"It should be. Harlan Kerrigan is a local land-owner. His son, Lonnie, was driving my truck when Mike was killed, and the family has feuded with the McClouds for generations." Chase paused, watching him. "Do you remember Mike?"

"No." Although I should, Trey thought.

"Mike was your older brother—and my best friend all through school. When we were seventeen, he was killed in a car wreck. I was in the pickup that hit him," Chase said bluntly. "And so was Lonnie. Your parents died a few years later."

Pieces of the story clicked into place. The dreams about funerals and cemeteries suddenly made sense to Trey.

"I can't tell Raine about the Rimes brothers," Chase continued. "If I do, she'll insist on going with me and when I refuse, she'll try looking on her own. This isn't like searching for you. This is dangerous. I don't want her hurt."

"Neither do I." It went against his every instinct to stay behind and let Chase hunt alone—but he'd only just found his sister. He couldn't let anything happen to her.

"Then I need your help." Swiftly Chase filled him in on his plan.

Trey wasn't sure Raine would ever forgive Chase for what he was about to do, but he was clearly determined, his face set in hard lines.

"This is the cell phone number for Andy Jones, the Agency bodyguard," Chase concluded, taking a slip of paper from his pocket and handing it to Trey. "If you don't hear from him by five o'clock, call him. He'll watch her house, but if you need him elsewhere, just tell him where and when."

Chase reached the doorway before Trey called his name—he paused, looking back at him.

"Just so we're clear," Trey said. "What exactly are your intentions toward my sister?"

"I plan to ask her to marry me just as soon as this is finished."

Trey grinned. "That's what I thought. Good luck."

Chase nodded and disappeared.

And he was going to need all the luck he could get, Trey thought. Chase was a bounty hunter, and Trey was confident that if anyone could catch Carl and Bobby Rimes, he could. But afterward, he'd have to come home and face Raine.

Chase was going to tell Raine they were finished and wouldn't see each other again. The news would make her furious, but would it keep her from asking the sheriff for an update on the case? What were the odds Raine could be kept in the dark until Chase brought in the Rimes brothers?

And would Raine take Chase back once she knew he'd lied to her? Trey wondered. He didn't remember all the details about his life, but he instinctively knew his sister was a smart, stubborn woman and she hated being deceived.

Just like Lori, he thought. Too bad I didn't realize all this earlier. Maybe I would have handled the situation better.

He picked up his bag and went into the bedroom. Like the living area, the room had a lofty ceiling and gleaming floor dotted with plush area rugs. A grouping of framed photos hung on the wall just inside the door. He dropped the duffel on a nearby chair and moved closer, studying the pictures. Two of them were snapshots of a family. He studied the faces, knowing with deep-seated certainty that here were his mother, father, Raine, himself and his older brother, Mike.

And except for himself and Raine, they were all gone. Mike in the car accident Chase had mentioned, and his parents a few years later. Though he felt sadness, he realized the grief was old and familiar, not fresh as if he'd just learned the truth. It was memory, not revelation.

It seemed being back home was indeed helping him remember more and more.

The bathroom had a walk-in shower big enough for four people. He stripped and washed up, recognizing the scent of his shampoo and soap.

"I need a haircut," he told the image in the foggy mirror when he rubbed a circle on the glass. He ran a brush through his hair before walking naked into the bedroom where he took faded jeans and a blue checked cotton shirt from the closet, then underwear from the dresser drawers.

He felt as if he were shedding the person he'd been since he woke up in the ditch and donning instead his own skin, as he tucked the shirt into his jeans and threaded a black leather belt through the loops.

The kitchen was well stocked, the sealed container of coffee beans right where he thought it would be in the cupboard. He automatically measured and ground them, filled the coffeemaker with water and switched it on.

A computer sat on a desk tucked beneath a window. While he waited for it to boot up, he thumbed through a neat stack of bills piled in a leather box nearby. The postmarks all had recent dates.

Raine must have been paying my bills.

Knowing that she cared for him and would have

done what was necessary to keep his world ticking over in his absence filled him with appreciation. Despite the still missing pieces of his memory, he had his life back, and it was clearly good.

He crossed the room to answer the quick rap on the door.

"Hi, come on in."

Raine studied him as she stepped inside. "I see you've decided to keep the beard."

He ran his palm over the day-old stubble. "Yeah, I've gotten used to it."

She headed for the kitchen and he dropped onto the sofa to pull on his boots.

"Maybe the girls will think it's sexy," she teased. "Did you make coffee?"

"It's in the carafe."

She took down a mug. "Ah," she sighed after sipping. "Now I *know* you're my Trey. Nobody brews coffee quite like you do."

He took a seat on the counter stool across from her. Her eyes were shadowed, her mouth had a vulnerable droop and he was pretty sure she'd been crying. *Aw, hell.* She obviously hadn't taken Chase's announcement well.

"I'm remembering more." He picked up his own mug and gestured at the copper pans and professional stove. "For instance, I'm a damn good cook, right?"

She laughed. "You're a fabulous cook."

Relieved when amusement lightened her face, changing the downward curve of her lips to an upward tilt, he drained his cup and carried it into the kitchen to slot it into the dishwasher.

"I'll take mine with me," she said, brandishing her mug. "I hate to admit it, but the restaurant coffee hasn't been the same without you there to supervise."

He grinned, pleased she seemed determined to put aside what must have been a difficult conversation with Chase. They spent a few moments discussing plans for the afternoon and how they were going to deal with his desire to keep news of his amnesia as quiet as possible. Now that he knew his identity and that of his attackers, he was more than ready to file a report with the sheriff. It would mean the local newspaper would want to do a story on him, but Raine agreed to sit in on any interviews.

"We'll need to tell Sam and Charlotte what's going on," Raine said. "But beyond the four of us, no one except the sheriff needs to know you can't recall everything."

"Who are Sam and Charlotte?"

"Charlotte is the assistant manager of the restaurant, and Sam has worked for us for years."

When they went downstairs, Sam had his back to them as he stacked empty bottles into a box at the near end of the bar. The stocky body and military-short white hair caught Trey off guard.

"Sam," Raine said.

Before he turned, Trey knew Sam's features as surely as his own. How could he not? he thought. Sam had been a second father to him and Raine when their own parents had fallen apart after Mike's death.

"Raine, I didn't know you were home. Did you find any new information at the—" His voice broke off as he caught sight of Trey.

"Hello, Sam." Trey wrapped his arms around the older man in a brief hard hug.

Sam returned the pressure with equal emotion and when he stepped back, his eyes were damp. "I'll be damned. I hardly recognized you with the stubble. Where the hell have you been?"

Trey waited to tell his story until Charlotte joined them and they were all together in the privacy of his office.

"So here I am, home again," he concluded at the

end of his tale. "Unfortunately, I'm still missing a good chunk of my memory—a fact I'd like to keep under wraps as much as possible."

"Why?" Charlotte asked, looking confused.

"Because the less attention I get for a while, the better. I'm guessing folks will be curious to know where I've been and my sudden return will cause enough of a stir. I'd rather not add to it with speculation about whether I'm brain-damaged from getting hit on the head."

"You're not, are you?" Sam looked at Trey with alarm.

"No," Trey assured him. "I've seen a doctor, two of them, as a matter of fact, and other than a scar and some gaps in what I remember, I'm fine."

"Great, that's good news," Sam said with relief.

"I don't think we need to make this complicated," Trey continued. "If you'll all back me up while I'm working and let me know people's names and what I should know about them, I doubt anyone will pick up on what's going on. And if I forget someone when none of you are around, I'll just say I have a killer headache, left over from getting knocked unconscious."

"So you want to let people know you were attacked?" Charlotte asked.

"Sure, the closer to the truth we stay, the easier it will be to keep our stories straight—and everyone is going to want to know where I've been. So we can tell them I was hijacked, hit over the head, and have been recovering in a hospital somewhere, how's that?"

"Works for me," Raine said. "In fact, the only thing we're not going to say is that you have partial amnesia, right?"

"Correct." Trey looked at Charlotte and Sam, and both nodded their agreement. "Good, that's settled, then." He pushed back his chair and stood. "I'm going to spend the rest of today and tonight in my apartment looking at photos, reading back issues of the local newspaper. In short, taking in as much information as I can about life here in Wolf Creek."

"Do you want us to tell people you're home?" Charlotte asked.

"No. I'll be back at work tomorrow. I'd like to stay as low-key as possible and folks will know I'm back soon enough."

"Okay." Sam nodded and got up. "I'd better get back to the bar and relieve Sheila." His face softened. "It's great to have you home, boy."

"Thanks, Sam. It's good to be back."

Charlotte threw her arms around him and hugged him tight. "Ditto from me, big guy. We've missed you!"

"Thanks."

"What can I do to help?" Raine said when the two had gone. "I'll bring dinner up from the restaurant—and how about the newspapers? I saved copies for you." She pointed at the bookcase in the corner where the bottom shelf held a stack of newsprint. "But when I was out of town searching for you, I'm pretty sure Sam tossed out the newer ones, since that pile hasn't grown."

"I'll read the ones I've got and scan the rest online. Do you have our high school yearbooks? The pictures might jog my memory and if they don't, you can tell me what I should know about our old friends and fill me in on what they're doing now, especially the ones I'm likely to run into."

They spent Trey's first night back home closeted in his apartment. Together they went through newspapers, photograph albums and high school yearbooks while Raine told him as much as she could about his life in Wolf Creek.

By ten o'clock they'd worked their way through all the albums and yearbooks. They were a third of the way through Raine's newspapers, piled next to the sofa. They both sat cross-legged on the floor, books and papers strewn around them.

"I need coffee." She rose, yawned, stretched and headed for the kitchen. "How about you?"

"Sure," he said absently as he took another newspaper off the stack. Across the bottom right quarter of the front page was a photo of a group of people, all posed with shovels at a construction site. He scanned the list of names below the picture and paused, stopped by one of them. "Harlan Kerrigan," he mused aloud. "So that's what he looks like."

"Let me see." Raine leaned over his shoulder and read the caption, then tapped the photograph with her forefinger. "Yes, that's him all right. Do you remember him?"

"He looks familiar but I only know what Chase told me, which wasn't much."

"What did Chase say about Harlan?"

"That the McClouds and the Kerrigans have been involved in a feud for a long time, Harlan owns land locally, and that his son, Lonnie, was involved somehow in the car crash that killed Mike."

"That's all?"

"Near as I can remember." Trey searched her face, curious. "Is there more?"

"There's always more when it comes to Harlan and Lonnie, but I think you have the basics." Raine pointed to the man standing next to Harlan in the photo. "This is Senator Clark. Over the last few years, Harlan's been spending a lot of time in Helena, making the rounds of the social functions and schmoozing government officials. The word is he's involved in several big deals, many of which wouldn't survive being exposed to daylight. He's contributed heavily to some senatorial campaigns, and gossip says the money is more bribe than political donation." Raine frowned at the picture. "Personally, I think there's more going on than anyone suspects. I wouldn't be surprised if Harlan has his sights set on a political career."

"What about Lonnie?"

"Lonnie's not a politician—he doesn't have the temperament. The only good thing I can say about him is that he's not as devious as his father. With Lonnie, all the bad stuff is up-front. Five minutes in his company and you know he's a bully and a braggart. He drinks too much, fights too much, and someday he's going to get himself into trouble that his father can't buy him out of."

"Nice family," Trey said dryly.

"Oh, yes," Raine said. "And Harlan has an office just a block away."

"Tell me what happened when you realized I was missing—what did you do?"

"I called the Sherriff's Office," Raine said. "But they couldn't find any information—it was as if you'd dropped off the face of the earth. So I drove out to Chase's ranch and demanded he help me find you."

"Just like that?" Trey looked at her, trying to read her expression. "And did he agree just as easily?"

"Not exactly." Raine waved a hand dismissingly.

"So he refused?"

"At first."

"How did you change his mind?"

"I told him you'd received an anonymous letter that might mean someone has information about the night Mike was killed."

"And that convinced him?" Trey said with surprise. He remembered clearly the day Chase had told him to forget the past and get on with his life. Hadn't he meant it?

"I think so. He certainly wasn't cooperative until he learned there may be new evidence."

"Hmmm." Trey noted the unhappy curve of Raine's mouth, a direct contrast to her brisk words and determined effort to conceal any reaction to Chase's name. He changed the subject, asking a question about a second photo on the newspaper's front page.

Trey insisted on driving her home just before midnight, telling her to humor him when she protested that she didn't need an escort. He waited until she waved good-night and went inside before driving off. He didn't go far. He parked around the block and dialed Andy Jones's cell phone number.

"Yo."

"This is Trey. I just left Raine at her house."

"I saw you," the professional bodyguard replied. "I'm in the blue van across the street out front. Chase's brother Luke is covering the alleyway in back."

"Thanks, man."

"No problem."

"How did you get from Seattle to Wolf Creek so fast?" Trey asked, curious.

"Private plane." There was a smile in his voice. "Grade-A Prime travel."

"How'd you swing that?"

"Chase has friends in high places. In this case, a software billionaire with a jet sitting on the ground at Boeing Field."

Trey rang off and went home, satisfied that Raine was being well watched.

The following morning brought a stream of longtime customers and friends into the saloon, stopping by to say hello to Trey and welcome him back. He worked in his office, coming out periodically to chat with people. To his relief he discovered he remembered quite a few of them, and when he didn't, Sam, Charlotte and Raine were quick to casually drop names and details.

Nevertheless, by the time the day ended and he could escape upstairs to his apartment, he'd had enough socializing. He thought about calling Lori and decided against it. She wasn't likely to talk to him and, in any case, he doubted he could convince her over the phone to forgive him. He still wasn't sure how he was going to accomplish that face-to-face.

But he would. Just as soon as Chase brought in the Rimes brothers and they learned who was behind the carjacking. Until he was sure being with her wouldn't endanger Lori, he had to stay in Wolf Creek.

And keep Raine safe, he thought. Fortunately, Andy Jones and Luke McCloud were taking the night shift while he kept watch on her during the day. With luck, she'd never know she was at risk.

Harlan Kerrigan dialed the phone with swift jabs, fury pounding at his temples.

"Yeah?"

"Trey Harper isn't dead," he snarled into the phone.

"What?" Shock filled Lonnie's voice.

"You heard me, he isn't dead. He's back in Wolf Creek and that sister of his is cozy with Chase McCloud." Harlan paced the plush Oriental carpet in his Helena home. "I want the Rimes brothers out of the country. Now. Before McCloud can find them and they have a chance to implicate me. Are they still in Wyoming?"

"I haven't talked to them in a day or two. I'll call and find out."

"Send them cash to buy one-way tickets to Belize and enough extra to live for a month. Tell them I want them out of the States and beyond McCloud's reach as soon as possible."

He punched the off button and threw the phone onto the desk. It gouged the fine cherrywood surface and bounced onto the floor.

The uneasy feeling that events were slipping out of his control enraged him. He stalked to the liquor cabinet and poured a shot of whiskey, downing it in one gulp.

Chapter Eight

Even a winning baseball team couldn't raise Lori's spirits. Despite her determination to put behind her the hours spent with Trey Harper and chalk them up as wasted time, she grieved.

At work, she met Kari and Ralph's concern with assurances that she was fine. In fact, she told them, she was relieved they'd all learned the truth before she'd become too involved with Trey. But when she went home at night, she dropped the bright facade she wore so determinedly all day.

The color had gone out of her life, taking with it

any semblance of the happy, fizzing excitement she'd felt with Trey, and left only dull shades of gray.

I will get over this, she told herself fiercely each morning as she dressed. *I will.*

Each evening that brought no word from Chase made Trey more impatient. His memory became stronger and more complete as the missing pieces of his life filled in the gaps, the process seemingly accelerated by the familiar surroundings of Wolf Creek.

His ability to recall details of the week prior to the carjacking, however, remained stubbornly blank.

Until the morning he helped Charlotte unload several boxes of office supplies from the back seat of her SUV. He stretched across the leather to reach a box on the floor and had an instant mental image of lying facedown on the carpeted floor of his own vehicle.

And hearing the voices of two men.

He stared at the carpet, laser-hot anger searing through him as he recalled their conversation.

"Trey? Can you reach it?" Charlotte asked from behind him. "I can fetch it from the other side."

"No, I've got it." He picked up the box and left

it for Charlotte to unpack and went looking for Raine. He found her in the utility room off the kitchen.

"Do you have a minute?"

She turned, the smile on her lips fading as she saw his expression. "Of course."

"Let's go in the office." He wanted privacy, with no chance of anyone overhearing.

"Is something wrong?" She looked worried, her gray eyes searching his face.

"I remembered something that might be important." He sat on the edge of the desk, one boot braced on the floor, determined not to frighten her. *Warn her. Don't scare her.* "Unfortunately, I'm not sure it's enough to get the sheriff involved."

"What is it?" She sat down in the leather armchair facing him, her gaze fixed on his.

"The two men who stopped when I was changing the flat tire were men I'd seen at an accident scene earlier. They were a couple of cars behind me, waiting for the state trooper to have a semi towed and clear the highway. We'd all been in a nearby motel office at the same time, getting coffee from the desk clerk."

"Did you have any inkling they might try to rob you?"

"No. They looked like ordinary cowboys after a day at work—dirty boots and jeans, beard stubble. After they threw me in the back of my SUV, I must have drifted in and out of consciousness, because I remember snatches of their conversation. One of them mentioned Lonnie Kerrigan."

Raine's eyes widened and she gasped.

Trey put his hand on her arm to reassure her then broached the critical question. "Have either Lonnie or Harlan approached or threatened you in any way?"

"Interesting you should ask," she said. "I rarely have dealings with either of them, but Harlan dropped by the office and Lonnie came into the saloon one night. Both of them made menacing comments about my hiring Chase to search for you."

"What about since I've been home?"

She shook her head. "I haven't seen or talked to either of them recently."

They discussed the two Kerrigan men for a while and then parted. Raine wanted him to promise not to challenge Harlan or Lonnie, but Trey stalled her, saying only he'd think about it.

He went upstairs to his apartment and dialed Luke's number.

"I need to talk to Chase," Trey said when he picked up.

"I don't know where he is—but I think he keeps in touch with Ren. Why?" Luke's voice sharpened.

"I remembered more about the carjacking. The two men who knocked me out used Lonnie Kerrigan's name."

Luke cursed. "I'll be damned. What's Lonnie got against you?"

"I don't know but it's looking more and more like whoever wanted to meet me at the Bull 'n' Bash has real evidence against Lonnie. Or Harlan," Trey answered. "And they both know it."

"It sure as hell does," Luke said grimly. "I'll call Ren and find out if he can reach Chase."

Damn good thing somebody can reach Chase, Trey thought as he hung up. Raine had told him Chase and Ren Colter were partners in a Seattle-based detective agency, Colter & McCloud Investigations. He couldn't help but think it was interesting that Chase had chosen Ren to be his contact person, rather than his brother Luke or his father, John.

He called Andy. After warning the bodyguard that Raine might be in more danger than they'd thought, he went back downstairs, determined not to let her out of his sight.

On Sunday he drove her to a barbecue at Chase's parents' house, where he had a chance to talk with Luke, his brother-in-law, Zach, and John, Luke and Chase's father. All three agreed with him that it was best to remain vigilant until Chase either called or returned.

They didn't have long to wait. The following evening, just as Trey hung up the phone after confirming that Andy was outside the saloon, waiting to follow Raine home, Chase knocked on his door.

"Damn, am I glad to see you. Come in."

Chase stepped over the threshold. Trey closed the door behind him.

"Did you find the Rimes brothers?"

"Yes." Chase scrubbed a hand down his face. "But I lost them in the Dakotas—they managed to get a flight to Belize."

"Hell." Trey swore with frustration. "Now what?"

"There's no use chasing them. I've been to Belize after other fugitives and it's damned near impossible to find them. We don't have time to spend months searching the jungle."

"So now what? We just give up? Harlan and

Lonnie get away with this, and Raine spends the rest of her life watching her back?"

A slow smile spread across Chase's face. "Oh, no," he drawled. "There's more than one way to stop Harlan, and Ren and I found one."

Intrigued, Trey studied him. Chase's expression was unashamedly satisfied. "Mind telling me what you did?"

"We found a way to blackmail him. I just left Harlan's office, where I told him that if he so much as blinked in Raine's direction in the future, I'd inform a certain senator about the affair Harlan's been having with his wife. I have photos—explicit photos."

"I'm impressed. How did you find out about this?"

"Through a disgruntled ex-lover who gave the pictures to a good friend of my mother." Chase looked at his watch. "It's getting late. I want to talk to Raine tonight, if she'll see me," he added.

"Good luck with that," Trey said dryly. "I doubt she's going to be easy to convince."

"Yeah, I was afraid of that."

Chase was halfway to the door before Trey remembered. "Did Ren give you the message about Lonnie?"

Chase stopped. "No. What about Lonnie?"

Trey explained and Chase's face took on a dangerous cast.

He stalked out of the apartment.

Trey let out a sigh. Now that Harlan and Lonnie had been effectively stopped and his sister was safe, he was free to return to Granger. And Lori. God, he missed her.

He looked at his watch. Too late to call tonight, he thought. I'll call tomorrow.

But the following morning he couldn't reach her. No one answered her home phone, she didn't respond to her cell, and she wasn't at her office.

Frustrated, he left the saloon and drove to the Wolf Creek Cemetery, where he'd promised to meet Chase and Raine.

Chase's announcement that Raine had agreed to marry him didn't surprise Trey. His next words, however, did.

"She said yes, if I could let go of the past. As of today, I'll stop searching for whoever wrote the letter you received. I'm going to concentrate on being Raine's husband and, hopefully, someday a father to our children. We thought it was fitting to tell Mike—" he cleared his throat "—to tell Mike what we're doing, and why, and ask for his blessing."

"You can't be serious?" Trey hadn't expected this. He glanced at the waist-high granite marker where his hand rested. Mike's gravestone was cold to the touch, despite the warmth of the day. "You're going to turn your back and walk away— never follow up on the only clue that might uncover what really happened to Mike?"

"I'm not saying I've forgotten how Mike died that night, nor that I wouldn't like to see Lonnie brought to justice. But I want a life with Raine more." Chase's voice rang with quiet conviction. "You need to let it go, too, Trey. Mike wouldn't want you to waste your life searching for proof that might not even exist."

Before Trey could argue, Raine spoke. "We want your blessing, too, Trey, as well as Mike's."

He realized instantly that there was nothing more to say. Raine needed this closure, deserved a chance to have a life out from beneath the sadness that had shadowed them for so long.

"You have it," he said. "Of all the people in the world, no one is more deserving of a chance to start married life free of old history."

Tears welled in her gray eyes and spilled over to track slowly down her cheeks. "Thank you, Trey," she said softly.

"I'm sure Mike would say the same." He stepped toward her and held out his arms. "Be happy," he whispered against her hair as he hugged her tight. Over her head his gaze met Chase's in silent understanding.

Harlan was beyond furious. He stared at the grainy copies of the photos taken of him and the senator's wife in bed.

How the hell had Chase McCloud gotten them?

His eyes narrowed as he calculated the odds that McCloud might get access to the other photos, the ones Sherry O'Connell claimed were taken fifteen years ago.

He strode across the office and yanked open the door. "Lonnie," he bellowed. "Get in here."

It was time to send Lonnie to Granger.

Trey spent the afternoon clearing off his desk and arranging for Sam, Charlotte and Raine to cover for him. Worried at first, their concern turned to smiles when they realized he was going back to Granger to court Lori.

He had a new SUV, purchased earlier in the week, and his bag was packed, loaded in the back by nine that night. But his plan to leave was thwarted when Luke and his sister Jessie's husband Zach arrived with John McCloud, Chase and Andy Jones.

"We've got a free evening, Trey." Luke carried a couple of six-packs of beer and Chase held a container of what smelled like barbecued chicken. "The women are at Dad's house, talking to Mom about holding Chase and Raine's wedding there. We were officially evicted and decided to hold an early bachelor party. Here."

Trey grinned. "Come on in."

An hour later, they were sprawled around the living room, watching a ball game on the flat-screen TV, drinking beer and arguing over whose team was going to win.

The phone rang and Andy, seated closest to it, picked it up.

"Yeah?" Pause. "Just a minute. Trey—it's for you."

"Who is it?" Trey asked as he levered himself off the sofa and crossed the room to take the phone.

Andy shrugged. "She didn't say."

It must be Raine, Trey thought, wondering if she was going to tell him he had to wear a tux to her wedding. "Hello."

"Trey? It's Lori."

* * *

At almost the same time that Trey was meeting Chase and Raine at the Wolf Creek Cemetery, Lori's cell phone rang in Granger.

That's odd, she thought, glancing at the Caller ID and recognizing her home phone number. Mom doesn't usually call me on my cell.

"Hi, Mom. What's up?"

"Lori." Risa's voice shook and was nearly inaudible. "Thank God I reached you."

"Mom?" She dropped the file she was holding and stood. "What's wrong?"

"A man—he forced his way into the house—he hit me…" Risa's voice broke on a sob.

Clutching the phone to her ear, Lori ran down the hall and through the archway.

"Butch," she called as she raced past the end of the long bar. "Call 911. I need an ambulance at the house." Lori barely registered Butch's alarm as he grabbed the phone before she was out the front door of the bar. She sprinted down the sidewalk.

"Mom? Are you there? Mom! Talk to me."

"I'm here. Are you coming home?"

"I'm on my way. Is the man still in the house?"

"No." Risa's voice wavered. "He left."

"Thank God," Lori said with relief, dragging in a long breath. "Did he hurt you?"

"He hit me—my lip is bleeding. He wrecked the living room."

"But you're not—hurt—otherwise?" Without looking, she ran onto the crosswalk, dodging the pickup truck that slammed on its brakes and slewed sideways to barely miss her.

"No."

"I'm almost there." The six blocks from downtown to home felt like six miles as Lori ran, trying to breathe and talk at the same time.

"Hurry."

She yanked open the screen door and flew into the house.

Risa sat curled on the sofa, the phone held to her ear. The shoulder of her dress was torn, her hair in disarray and she was missing one shoe.

Lori's heart clenched, fearing the worst.

"Mom?" She knelt in front of the sofa and tried to take Risa's free hand in hers. "Are you sure you're okay? He didn't hurt you?"

"He broke my necklace." Risa lowered the phone from her ear and held out her other hand, opening her fist to reveal a handful of loose pearls. "The one your father gave me."

"It's okay, Mom, we'll fix it." Lori fought to keep the panic from her voice as she scanned Risa's face. Her lip was puffy and there was a small cut at one corner, but other than that, she couldn't see any obvious damage.

Sirens wailed in the street outside. Within seconds, two emergency medical technicians appeared at the screen door.

"Medic One." The male voice was deep, reassuring.

"Come in," Lori called over her shoulder.

"What happened?" An EMT knelt beside her, opening his bag.

"She says a man broke into the house and attacked her," Lori told him.

"If you'll move aside, Lori, we'll take a look."

"Of course." Lori did as they asked. Ben, the older of the two paramedics was in his forties, and Lori had known him since she was fourteen and broke her collarbone falling off the swing at the park.

"Morning, Risa," Ben said to her mother, his voice soothing. "Let's take a look at that lip. Are you having pain anywhere else?"

Lori paced away from the sofa to the window and back, hugging herself, listening closely as the two men assessed Risa.

"She'll be fine. We won't take her to the hospital tonight but you might want to schedule an appointment with her regular physician tomorrow so he can give her a thorough exam," Ben told Lori while his partner repacked the bag. "Do you want me to call her doctor and ask him to prescribe something to calm her and help her sleep tonight?"

"Thanks, Ben, but she has sedatives the doctor gave her after Dad passed away. I'll have her take one before she goes to bed, unless you think she should have one sooner?"

"Your call—or hers, if she feels she needs one."

A Sheriff's Office car stopped out front.

Ben glanced out the window. "Reid's here. I'll just let him in—why don't you go to your mom."

Lori nodded her thanks and went to sit next to Risa on the sofa. Her mother looked up and smiled wanly when the sheriff entered.

"My goodness. First the ambulance, now a sheriff's car parked outside the house—the neighbors will be gossiping for weeks."

"They're just jealous because their lives are so boring, Risa," Reid chided her gently. "What happened here?"

For the first time since racing through the front

door, Lori took in the condition of the living room. Drawers from the antique writing desk were tipped upside down on the floor, their contents spilled onto the carpet. From her seat on the couch, she had a clear view into the dining room and further destruction.

"He went upstairs and I heard him ransacking the bedrooms." Risa twisted her hands together, her face paling.

"What was he looking for? Did he tell you?"

Risa nodded, her eyes full of misery as she looked at Lori. "He said he wanted the copies of the photos. I told him I didn't know what he was talking about, but he wouldn't listen. He just kept pulling out drawers and dumping everything."

Lori shook her head, disoriented. "What photos, Mom?"

"The photos Sherry gave me before she left town. Remember, I told you Sherry had to go away and she asked me to do her a favor?"

Lori nodded. "Yes, I know, but what does that have to do with the man who hit you?"

"He wanted the photos in the envelope Sherry left with me. It wasn't supposed to be him, Lori. Sherry said she wrote and told Trey to come get them."

"Trey?" Lori couldn't seem to grasp what her

mother was telling her. "Are you saying Trey Harper had something to do with the man who attacked you?"

"No, no." Risa fluttered her hands, becoming more agitated. "Sherry sent Trey a letter and told him to come to Granger and she'd give him the photos, but then she had to leave town. So she called and left a message on his machine to tell him he should see me instead. But then the awful man arrived and started tearing up the house."

"Do you understand any of this?" Reid asked Lori.

"I'm afraid not." She shook her head. "I've noticed Sherry has seemed stressed and worried over the past few months but I thought it was because her sister was so ill."

"Breast cancer," Risa interjected, her face sad. "She passed away several weeks ago."

"I remember," Reid said. "Must have been hard on the family, losing her like that."

"Sherry seemed to take it especially badly," Lori agreed.

"She was devastated," Risa said. "Sherry wanted to take her to a treatment clinic in Mexico, but at the last minute, she couldn't get cash. It was very expensive, over a quarter of a million dollars, but she truly believed it would save her sister." Risa sighed. "And then her sister died. Sherry blames the man who refused to give her the money."

"It's terribly sad," Lori agreed, patting her mother's hand. "But what's the connection between Sherry, the envelope with photos she gave you, Trey Harper, and the man who broke into our house?"

"I have no idea." Risa looked as bewildered as Lori felt.

They both stared at Reid.

The sheriff lifted his hands and let them drop, shaking his head. "Neither do I. But it bears looking into, since it appears the envelope is what the man was looking for. Would you recognize him if you saw a photo of him, Risa?"

"I think so."

"Good. Why don't you come by the station sometime tomorrow afternoon and go through the wanted posters. Maybe we'll get lucky."

"Of course. I'd be glad to."

"In the meantime, I'm going to assign a deputy to keep watch outside your house in a patrol car tonight. I doubt your attacker will return, but I'm sure you'll feel safer with an officer nearby." He left with their grateful thanks, promising to contact them the moment he had any information.

"Would you like to lie down, Mom? Or can I make you some tea?"

"Tea would be nice, Lori."

Risa's movements lacked their usual energy, and she lowered herself gingerly into a chair at the small table beneath the window looking out on the garden. She smoothed her hair and fingered her torn shoulder seam. "I must look awful."

"No, you don't," Lori assured her, turning to inspect her mother while filling the kettle. "You look fabulous, as always."

She was rewarded with a pale imitation of Risa's normal laugh. The sound was muted, but it was definitely a chuckle, Lori thought with relief.

"Thank you, dear. I don't know what I'd do without you. I don't tell you often enough how much I appreciate you."

"Oh, Mom." Lori's heart lurched when Risa's eyes filled with tears and she dropped her face into her hands. Leaving the kettle half-filled on the counter, she rushed across the room to wrap her mother in a hug. "It's going to be all right, Mom," she soothed. "Reid will catch this person and we'll get to the bottom of whatever's going on, I promise."

Risa held on tight for a moment, then eased back. "I know we will. I have faith in Reid." She cupped Lori's cheek. "And in you." She drew in a deep breath. "Now, about that tea."

They drank their tea at the sunny kitchen table, Lori listening as Risa described her latest trip to Billings.

"I think you should draw him."

Risa's comment came out of the blue, startling Lori, who'd been listening to a description of the romantic comedy Risa and her friend had taken in at the movie theater.

"Draw who?"

"The man." Risa's eyes lit with purpose. "I can tell you what he looks like and you can sketch him, just like those police artists do on TV."

"I don't know," Lori said doubtfully. "I'm not sure I can—police sketch artists are specially trained."

"But you're very good at drawing people," Risa insisted. "Let's try it."

Not wanting to upset her, Lori let Risa urge her into the closet where she'd packed away her pencils and sketch pads. They returned to the kitchen where the light was good, and began.

Two hours and several pots of tea later, Risa

leaned over Lori's shoulder. "Yes, that's him. No doubt about it," she said triumphantly. "I knew you could do it. You're a wonderful artist, Lori."

"Mmm," Lori responded, distracted by the face she'd drawn on the pad. It was almost handsome, though a certain air of dissipation was implicit in the heavy lines of cheeks and jaw. Lori didn't recognize him, but with luck, the sheriff, or Trey, would.

"Let's take it to Reid's office now, Mom," she said, picking up the pad. "Maybe it's not as precise as a photo, but hopefully he can use it." *And I'll ask him to make a copy for me so I can send it to Trey.* She couldn't help but wonder if the mystery surrounding Trey being hijacked was connected to the attack on Risa.

That evening, Lori waited until her mother was asleep before telephoning Trey. She left the office door ajar, in case Risa woke and needed her. Tucking the phone between shoulder and ear, she dialed information and slipped the copy of her drawing onto the scanner, closing the lid just in time to jot down Trey's phone number.

It took only a few moments to scan the drawing, save it to a file and attach it to an e-mail. Then she dialed Trey.

"Yeah?"

Startled, she paused. "Hello. I'm trying to reach Trey Harper."

"Just a minute." The strange male voice was less clear as he said, "Trey, it's for you."

She could make out the rise and fall of men's voices and what sounded like the clink of glasses.

"Hello."

She drew in a sharp breath, only now realizing she'd needed to hear his voice ever since Risa had called her cell phone earlier that day. She felt instantly safer.

"Trey, it's Lori."

"Lori? Where are you?"

"I'm in Granger. Something happened to Mom today and I need you to…"

"Hold on a second. It's noisy here. I'm going into the next room." The sound faded and she heard a door slamming. "Tell me that again—what about your mom?"

"A man broke into the house today and terrified Risa."

He bit off a curse. "Is she hurt?"

"She's more scared than anything. He slapped her across the face and bruised her cheek. She also has a small cut by her mouth, but other than that, she isn't harmed. He trashed the house, though."

"Damn. I'm sorry, honey. Did you call the sheriff?"

Lori ignored the rush of pleasure at his use of the endearment. "Yes, Reid was here and he took a statement. That's why I'm calling. Apparently, the man was looking for some photos Mom was holding for a friend. The friend told her she'd called and left a message for you to come pick them up."

"What?"

The obvious surprise in his voice reassured Lori that he hadn't known Risa was in danger.

"That's what Mom said. I don't know what connection, if any, there could possibly be between you and this man, but if there is one, I'm hoping you'll recognize him. Mom gave me a description, and I've sketched a face that she says is a good likeness. I want to e-mail it to you but I don't have your address."

He gave it to her and she tucked the phone against her shoulder as she quickly typed it in and hit the send button.

"It's on its way," she told him. "Will you call me back and tell me if you know him?"

"Don't hang up," he said quickly. "I'm going into the living room to check my computer."

Abruptly, the sound of voices grew louder.

"Hey, quiet you guys. I'm on the phone." Trey's words were muffled as though he'd covered the mouthpiece with his hand.

"Got it," he said in her ear, his voice normal again. "It's downloading."

She waited impatiently.

He swore, his voice grim.

"What is it?" she demanded.

"Where are you?"

"At home."

"Is Risa there, too?"

"Yes, she's upstairs asleep."

"I want you to hang up the phone and call the sheriff, tell him you need him, right now. Then call me back."

"Wait—don't hang up—there's a deputy outside the house. Reid has him spending the night there."

"Thank God." The relief in his voice was palpable.

"Trey, you know him, don't you?"

"Oh, yeah, I know him. We grew up in the same town. His name is Lonnie Kerrigan. I can't prove it yet, but I'm sure he hired the two men who hijacked my car and tried to kill me."

"And now he's attacked my mother. Why? Mom's never seen him before and neither have I— why would he want to hurt her?"

Chapter Nine

"I don't know, honey, but we'll find out. I want you to walk outside and tell the deputy I need to talk to him. Have him come back inside with you."

The living room had gone silent as Trey talked. Someone had muted the television, the picture flickering as the game silently continued on the screen.

They all listened as Trey told the deputy the identity of Risa's attacker, then asked him to inform the sheriff and remain with Lori and her mother.

"I'm on my way," he said when Lori was back

on the phone. "The deputy is going to stay with you until I get there. Don't leave the house without him."

She murmured agreement and he hung up. All five men watched him, waiting.

"Lonnie broke into Lori's house and ransacked it. Her mother was home at the time—she's safe, but he scared her. I'm going to go get them both and bring them back here until we can figure out what the hell the Kerrigans are up to now."

"I'll go with you," Chase said.

"Me, too," Luke added. "Dad, do you and Zach want to stay in town and make sure Mom and the rest of the women are safe?"

John nodded. "You're welcome to bring Lori and her mother out to the ranch, Trey. Harlan won't have the nerve to come anywhere near there."

"Thanks, John."

Ten minutes later, the vehicles blocking the alley below Trey's apartment sped away—Zach, John and Andy heading toward the McCloud headquarters while the two black SUVs, Chase and Luke in one, Trey in the other, raced northeast to Granger.

"They're here."

The deputy's voice roused Lori, and she threw

back the afghan, swinging her legs off the sofa as she sat up. She ran her fingers through her hair, pushing the heavy mass behind her ears while she walked to the window. Two black SUVs were just pulling up to the curb in front of the house, headlights going dark as the engines switched off.

A man got out of the lead vehicle and stalked swiftly toward the house. She recognized Trey instantly, his long legs quickly covering the distance between street and porch. Chase and another man exited the second vehicle and followed him.

The deputy unlocked the door and let them in, the low murmur of deep male voices reaching her in the living room.

"Where is she?"

"Lori's in there," the deputy said. "Her mother's upstairs asleep."

Trey entered the living room, barely pausing before he saw her in the shadows by the window. He strode over and grabbed her, his arms wrapping her, pressing her tight against his big body.

"I know you're mad at me," he said in a hoarse whisper. "Call truce. I need to know you're okay. Just let me hold you for a minute."

Lori squeezed her eyes shut and burrowed against him. For the first time since she'd gotten that terrifying call from Risa, the stress and strain of worry and fear lifted and she let herself be comforted.

"Lori?" Her mother's voice broke the spell that bound her. "What's going on? It's the middle of the night."

Lori stirred, pushing against Trey's arms, and the moment of peace between them was over. She stepped around him, avoiding his eyes as she joined Risa. "I know, Mom. It's all right. Trey and his friends have come to take us somewhere safe until the sheriff arrests the man who hit you."

"But I don't want to go anywhere," Risa protested, confusion on her face, her features still sleepy. "Why should I be forced out of my home because of a criminal?"

"John and Margaret McCloud have invited you to come to Wolf Creek until this is resolved, Mrs. Ashworth," Trey said gently. "We'll remain here, of course, if that's what you want, but I thought you might enjoy visiting them at their ranch."

Risa's face brightened. "Oh, that's different. Why didn't you tell me the McClouds had invited us to stay with them, Lori? I'll just go upstairs and pack a bag."

She did an abrupt about-face and marched back up the stairs.

Lori sighed and looked at Chase. "This is very kind of your parents, Chase." She tipped her head slightly as she looked past him at Luke. "You must be a McCloud, too."

"This is my brother Luke. And my folks are looking forward to having your mother as their guest."

Trey was grateful Lori appeared to be too tired to pick up on Chase's phrasing. He'd told the McClouds that Lori would be staying with him at his apartment while Risa was at John and Margaret's home. He didn't plan on breaking the news to Lori until they reached Wolf Creek. He knew she'd probably argue and say no. He, on the other hand, refused to let her out of his sight. It was his fault violence had invaded her life. He vowed it wouldn't happen again, even if he had to keep her chained to his side until Lonnie was arrested and safely locked away.

Lori wanted to ride with her mother, until he explained that if she went with Trey, Risa would have the entire back seat of Chase's SUV to lie down and sleep. She fussed over her mother, tucking a soft afghan over Risa's lap, before reluctantly joining Trey. Shortly after they left Granger, Lori fell asleep.

The clock was inching slowly toward morning but all about them the night was pitch-black, except for the cone of light the headlights cast on the highway ahead of them. Chase's SUV followed closely behind Trey's. All three men had handguns tucked into the storage compartments between the front passenger seats. If Lonnie had plans for further trouble, they were prepared.

By the time Trey reached his parking slot behind the saloon in Wolf Creek, the dark sky was turning to gray.

He switched off the engine and got out, stretching to eliminate the kinks from the long drive before taking their bags from the back and handing them to Chase. Leaving his vehicle running, lights on, Chase took Trey's keys and disappeared inside.

Moments later he returned and dropped the keys in Trey's palm. "The apartment's clear. Andy's downstairs, patrolling the bar and restaurant."

"Thanks, Chase."

"No problem. Get some sleep. See you tomorrow."

Chase and Luke waited while he gently shook Lori awake and half carried her into the building.

He heard the low rumble of the engine fading away as they went up the stairs.

"This can't be the McCloud ranch." Lori's drowsy eyes lost their sleepy, half-lidded appearance as she looked about her.

"It's not." Trey took her arm and towed her with him into the bedroom.

"Then where are we?" she demanded suspiciously.

"This is my place." He pulled back the blankets on the bed, grabbing one of the pillows. "You're sleeping here." He opened the closet and snagged a throw from the top shelf. "I'll be sleeping on the sofa."

She was still standing where he'd left her, arms crossed, her chin set at a stubborn angle.

He walked past her and stopped in the doorway. "The bathroom's through there." He pointed. "You've got ten minutes to get your pajamas on and climb into bed. If you don't, I'll take it as an invitation to join you."

"Why are you doing this?"

"Because I want you safe. If I have to padlock you to me until Lonnie's caught and you're out of danger, that's what I'll do." The thought of what might have happened if she'd been in the house when Lonnie burst in made his blood chill. "I know you don't like it. And I know you're mad as hell at me. When this is over, you can yell all you want, but in the meantime, cut me some slack. Let me do this for you."

She stared at him, her eyes huge and shadowed, darkened to nearly emerald. "All right," she acceded finally. "We'll call a ceasefire until Lonnie's caught."

"Thank you." His voice rasped, roughened by emotion. He stood still, fighting the need to go to her. "It's late," he said finally.

She murmured good-night.

He turned off the lamp in the living room and tossed the bedclothes on the sofa. A wave of weariness hit him as he took the handgun from the small of his back where he'd tucked it into his waistband, and laid it on the coffee table. He pulled his T-shirt off over his head and dropped it next to the weapon. He normally slept in his boxers, but in deference to Lori, he left his jeans on, dropping onto the sofa to pull off his boots.

The strip of light beneath the bedroom door went dark and he lay down, pulling the blanket up to his waist. Despite tiredness that dragged at his bones and sanded his eyes, he stared at the ceiling, savoring the knowledge that Lori slept in his bed.

Too bad I can't be with her, he thought. He yawned and closed his eyes, sleep finally towing him under.

The sun was just starting to come up when the muffled screams woke him. He sat bolt upright, palming the gun as he leaped off the sofa and ran into the bedroom. There was just enough light in the room to see Lori pulling at the blankets with clenched fists, her head twisting against the pillow. Eyes closed, she struggled in the midst of a nightmare.

Trey laid his weapon on the bedside table and bent over her.

"Lori," he said softly. "Wake up. You're having a bad dream."

She moaned, still caught in the imaginary horror, and he shook her gently.

"Lori."

She came awake with a rush, sitting up suddenly, her eyes wide and terrified. "What?"

"Shh," he murmured. "It's okay. You had a nightmare."

"Oh." She wilted, falling back onto the pillow. "You're here." Deep relief vibrated in her voice.

"Yes, I'm here." He smoothed the tangle of platinum hair off her forehead. "You okay now?"

She nodded but her hands still gripped the edge of the covers and her body was rigid with fear.

"You sure you're all right?"

"Yes." Her voice was firm, but her fingers didn't loosen.

He left her reluctantly, admiring her pluck but wishing she wasn't so stubborn.

A half hour later, her cries woke him again.

This time he took his pillow and blanket into the bedroom along with the gun.

She woke as he entered, jerking upright in a panic.

"Oh, it's you." She covered her eyes with both hands, then swept her hair back, her fingers trembling. "I keep having the same dream. A man without a face is attacking Mom and I can't reach her in time."

"Don't worry about it. I've had a few bad dreams lately, myself." He put his gun down.

"I'm sorry I woke you. I don't think I can sleep without having another nightmare. Maybe I'll read for a while." She reached for the lamp.

Trey stopped her, catching her hand and tucking it back under the blanket. "No. You're exhausted— probably part of the reason you're waking up. Move over."

"I don't think…"

"Good, don't," he interrupted. "Just for the record, I'm going to sleep on top of your cover and under my own." He dropped the pillow on the mattress and slid down beside her, shaking out the blanket over his legs. He closed his eyes and lay still, waiting.

"I know what you're up to," she warned him finally. "And it's not going to work."

He smiled. "Okay. *It* won't work, whatever *it* is. But for now, we're going to sleep."

He woke the next morning and automatically reached for Lori. He was alone; her side of the bed was empty. The aroma of coffee made his nose twitch and he rolled over, stopping when he saw Lori.

She was curled in a chair, a mug cradled in her hands, watching him.

"Good morning," he said gruffly, yawning. The sight of her made him grin.

"What's so amusing?" she asked, lifting one eyebrow.

"Nothing. It's just nice to see you here, in my bedroom. It would be even better if you came back to bed," he suggested.

"That's not going to happen." She stood and set the coffee mug on the bedside table. "Your sister called earlier. Chase and Luke want us to drive out to their parents' ranch as soon as you're awake. Evidently, all of the McClouds are gathered there."

He nodded, pushing up to sit against the headboard. He picked up her coffee to steal a mouthful and, over the top of the mug, he watched the sway of her hips as she left the room.

It's going to happen. You're just not ready to give in yet. But soon.

He threw back the blanket and headed for the shower.

An hour later, they were on their way to the McClouds'. Trey had spent the time questioning Lori about her mother's version of why Lonnie had been in their house.

Risa and the rest of the women spirited Lori away the moment they got there.

Though reluctant to let her out of his sight, Trey used the opportunity to ask the McClouds to gather in John's office. Luke and Chase arrived first, joining their father and Trey.

"What's going on?" Chase asked.

"Let's wait for Zach so I don't have to go over the details twice," Trey said.

Luke looked thoughtful. "This is starting to sound like a war council."

Trey didn't laugh. "It is."

Chase and Luke exchanged a glance but didn't comment.

Zach was the last to enter the room.

"Lock the door, will you? I don't want anyone walking in on us."

Zach looked curious but did as Trey asked. "Okay, we're all here. What's going on?"

"I think I've found proof Harlan was at the accident scene the night Mike died."

All four men went still.

"What kind of proof?" Chase asked.

"Photos." Trey paced up and down as he related what Lori had told him about Risa's statement to the sheriff.

"So the photos are gone?" Chase asked, his face grim.

Trey nodded.

"Damn." Now it was Luke's turn to prowl the room.

"What makes you so sure the photos were of Mike's accident?" John asked.

"Why else would she ask Risa to give them to me? My only connection with the Kerrigans is Mike's death. And Sherry told Risa her sister was involved in an affair with a rich man from Wolf Creek five years ago."

"No other way to find out what was in the photos?" Zach put in.

"Not that I know of," Trey responded. "Risa said her friend had told her there were photos in the envelope Lonnie took. As soon as we find her, we can ask her, but Risa swears Sherry never mentioned copies."

"Well, that's that." Luke leaned against the doorjamb, frustration evident in every line of his body.

"Maybe not," Trey muttered, thinking aloud.

All four men eyed Trey.

"You've got an alternative plan?" Chase said, his voice as expressionless as his face.

"My daddy always said there's more than one way to skin a cat. Some criminals are caught and do the time for the crime. Others get nailed for smaller mistakes. Take Al Capone—he was notorious for murder, extortion and bootlegging but the FBI didn't take him down for any of that. They got him for income tax evasion."

"You're saying Harlan's been cheating on his income tax?" Chase asked, one eyebrow lifting.

"Not that I know of, although I wouldn't put it past him." Trey looked at Zach. "I'm saying he cheated on something else. Something worth millions. Something that qualifies for grand larceny, not petty theft."

Zach went still. "You think we can prove Harlan embezzled from my grandfather's estate?"

"Yeah."

"Okay," Chase said slowly. "Tell us how."

"Raine told me Harlan is compulsive about documenting everything—in fact, he's obsessive about it. She noticed the trait in his involvement with the Chamber of Commerce. I'm betting he kept all the paperwork connected to draining money out of your grandfather's estate before Marcus died, Zach."

"Yeah, but where?" Luke put in. "How would we find it or even access it if we did know? If Harlan filed everything, it could be in a bank box in Wolf Creek or Helena, or some other town. Or it could be at his office, his home or out at the ranch house. Hell, for all we know, he could have buried it somewhere. Where do we start looking?"

"I'm hoping you, Zach or your sister, Rachel, can help us figure that out," Trey said. "Your mother, sister and you stayed with Marcus after your dad died. Harlan and Lonnie lived there, too. I know the house is big and you've said you avoided both of them as much as possible, but I'm hoping you saw enough of your uncle to make a guess about where he might put something he wanted to keep secret."

Zach frowned at the floor, obviously deep in thought. Then he shifted suddenly, his gaze lifting. "The house," he said slowly. "When I was thirteen, Granddad installed a walk-in security vault in his bedroom for his antique gun collection. Mom told me Harlan took over the room after Granddad moved to the nursing home. His will left the weapons to me but Harlan claims Granddad sold them to raise cash to cover bad investments."

"How large is the vault?" Chase asked. "Is it only deep enough to mount the guns on the wall? Or is it bigger?"

"It's maybe six feet wide by four feet deep. Harlan and Lonnie were out of town when the workmen installed it but I was home so I hung around and watched them."

"And the door? What kind of lock?" Trey queried.

"You can't see the door itself—it looks like all the other walls in the room. When you key in the right combination of numbers on a fingerpad, a whole panel slides sideways, like a pocket door." Zach paused. "It's directly across from the hall door and lined with mirrors."

"What's the likelihood Harlan would keep incriminating evidence in a family vault? Wouldn't he be smart enough to know that's the first place you'd look?" Luke said, his expression unconvinced.

"I doubt he thinks anyone but he and Marcus knew it existed. Grandad was very secretive about it, and no one was scheduled to be home when he had it installed, including me. I was supposed to spend the week at a friend's house, but his family had an emergency and canceled."

"And Harlan never found out you were there?"

"I don't think so. He was gone for a few weeks and by the time he came home, my canceled visit was old news. Not that he would have asked," Zach added. "He had no interest in anything Rachel and I did unless it involved Lonnie."

"Okay, if Harlan thinks no one knows about the vault, then maybe it's the most likely place he'd hide the information," Luke conceded.

"Exactly what kind of documents are we looking for?" Chase put in.

"Cash transactions." Zach's expression was grim. "Harlan was careful to provide the estate attorney with documents signed by Granddad while he was in the nursing home verifying he'd transferred property and sold stock. There were hundreds of deals and the few I've had time to trace have a money trail that's convoluted and complicated. So far I haven't been able to find proof the end result generated profit rather than loss, but I'm convinced it's there."

"So it's possible that if we follow the money we might get proof Harlan manipulated the books?"

Zach nodded. "I think so. But it'd be a helluva lot faster if we can find a set of duplicate books that covers the last few years."

"Good." Luke looked at Zach, his eyes glinting. "So, how do we get into the house?"

"That won't be difficult," Zach said. "Harlan and Lonnie are both in Helena this week for hearings on a water rights bill. The biggest problem is deciphering the code to open the vault."

"I'll call Ren," Chase said.

"How will Ren get it?" Luke asked, clearly puzzled and intrigued.

"If there's a security code, it's registered somewhere, maybe with the company that installed it. If Ren can't hack into their computer and find it, he can get us the schematics for the system Marcus had installed and tell us how to crack it."

"Damn." Zach whistled. "Gotta love a guy that good at breaking and entering."

Chase looked amused. "Speaking of breaking and entering, we're going to be guilty of the crime ourselves the minute we enter Harlan's house."

Luke shrugged. "Who cares? If the evidence is there, Harlan isn't going to be in any position to file a police report."

"True." Trey grinned at him.

John, who'd been listening without comment, finally spoke. "If you obtain evidence illegally, can you use it in a court of law?"

"Probably not," Chase admitted.

"Then I suggest we find another way. Lonnie's finally stepped over the line and committed a crime that has a good chance of sending him to prison." John's face hardened. "I want the same for Harlan." He held up his thumb and forefinger, almost but not quite touching. "We're this close to putting both of them away and severing Harlan's hold on this county. Let's not blow it."

Reluctantly the others agreed with him. Much as they wanted to raid Harlan's house, they had to concede it would be better if they found evidence legitimately.

Trey was quiet on the drive home, and Lori wondered what the conference in John's office had been about. Using the excuse that she was still tired, she went into the bedroom as soon as they entered the apartment.

He let her go without comment but she felt the weight of his gaze between her shoulder blades as she walked away. The tension between them thickened the air and she wondered how long before it exploded.

Much as she denied it, she knew in her heart of hearts that she wanted him.

She didn't trust him; after all, he'd lied to her.

But she craved the blind passion that she felt when he kissed her. No one but Trey had stirred that in her...what if no one else ever did again?

She slid off her jeans, folding them on the bed. Then she tugged the green cotton camisole over her head, piling it neatly on top of her Levis. She moved the clothes to the end of the dresser, planning to shower. But she was distracted by the framed photos on the wall. She'd looked at them earlier this morning, but hadn't had time to really study them. Now she did, and was fascinated by the window on Trey's childhood. She leaned closer to the picture of Trey, Raine and their parents.

How sad that he and his sister are the only ones left in their family.

The door opened. Wearing only jeans, Trey took one stride into the room and stopped abruptly. His eyes narrowed, going hot as they skimmed her body from head to toe, then returned for a slower second appraisal.

Heat moved up her throat, burning along her cheekbones, as she realized she wasn't wearing anything but a lacy pale green bra and panties.

"Sorry." His voice was deeper, roughened. "I came in to get a pillow and blanket—I thought you were in the shower."

"I almost am." She refused to flutter like a schoolgirl and forced her hands to remain at her sides when she desperately wanted to cover herself.

His gaze met hers. "How far does this truce of ours go?"

Desire flickered and raced through her veins, pooling in her belly and moving lower. Her nipples hardened, the lace of her bra faintly abrasive against the sensitive tips.

"I don't know what you mean." It was a last, desperate attempt to fight herself, and him.

He knew it. He reached her in two long strides.

"Yes, you do." He lifted his hand and caressed her cheek, his thumb stroking the swell of her bottom lip. "I want you, Lori."

"You lied to me," she muttered, wincing at the undercurrent of pain she couldn't erase from her voice.

"I did," he agreed. "And I'll regret it the rest of my days."

"I don't trust you."

Now he was the one who flinched, hurt and remorse clouding in his eyes. "I'll have to change that."

"Just because we sleep together doesn't mean I care about you," she said.

His eyes darkened with intent. He slipped his arms around her waist and slowly gathered her against him. "Liar," he whispered just before his mouth took hers.

His body was sleek and hot. Lori clasped his neck and pulled him closer, reveling in the slide of her bare skin against his. The soft denim of his jeans gently abraded the inside of her legs as he cupped her bottom and lifted her, fitting the cove of her hips against the harder angles of his.

She murmured and twisted in a vain attempt to get closer, and he nudged her backward until the edge of the mattress met her legs. Then they were falling, rolling on the bed until he was on top of her.

Yes, she thought. This was what she wanted—his weight blanketing her, his lips on hers. She stroked her hands down his back, and his muscles shifted, shuddering in reaction.

He kissed the underside of her chin, moving down her throat to linger on the pound of her pulse at the base of her neck. He slipped her bra straps off her shoulders, nudging the lacy cups aside until his mouth closed over her nipple.

She arched against him, breathless, and he sat up, stripping off his jeans and pausing a second to tear open a silver packet before he returned.

"Baby…" His voice was guttural as he unhooked her bra and slid her undies down her legs. "Next time we'll go slower, I promise."

She wondered hazily what he meant but then he kissed her again, his mouth hot against hers as he nudged against her center, demanding entrance. She surged toward him, desperate to have him inside her, and he slid home. He groaned, holding himself rigidly still for a moment. She pulled him closer and he cursed softly and began to move, quickly driving her crazy and sending them both over the edge.

They made love several times, agreeing wordlessly to set aside the unresolved issues that still lay between them.

The following morning everything conspired to put off the conversation they both knew was inevitable. First Trey was called downstairs after breakfast to deal with a bar delivery mix-up. Then Risa phoned and chatted with Lori for two hours. After that, Raine ran upstairs planning to discuss her wedding with Trey but spending most of the time brainstorming with Lori.

The interruptions were seemingly endless and by dinnertime, they still hadn't managed to talk about the night before and what it meant to their future.

At six o'clock, just when Lori thought the evening would bring quiet time and conversation, Raine and Chase arrived, with Zach and his wife, Jessie, and Luke and Rachel.

Lori would have given anything for three hours alone with Trey.

Chapter Ten

"I don't think Harlan would have left evidence lying about. He's too cagey for that," Raine argued. The remnants of dinner, ordered and delivered from the restaurant downstairs, were scattered over the countertop and coffee table.

"Locking something inside a wall safe isn't the same as leaving it out in the open. He has no reason to believe anyone would ever find out. And remember," Zach added, "he doesn't realize anyone else knows the safe exists."

"But still—by keeping the documents he risks

possible exposure. Why wouldn't he destroy them?" Lori asked, clearly unconvinced.

"Because he's obsessive about keeping note of details. He always has been," Zach explained. "Granddad was the same—he kept two sets of books, always, in case there was a fire at the office and the originals were destroyed."

"But those were legitimate business records, weren't they? Having a backup makes perfect sense for a company, but if you're committing a crime, would you keep written proof of illegal transactions?" Raine shook her head. "It just seems reckless and stupid. And I've never thought Harlan was dumb."

"Lonnie, on the other hand, isn't the brightest bulb," Chase said dryly. "Stupid and Lonnie go hand in hand."

Everyone laughed.

"That doesn't mean he isn't dangerous," Trey cautioned. "We shouldn't underestimate him."

"No," Chase agreed. "You're right. He's more than capable of violence."

"So, where does that leave us?" Trey asked.

The room was silent.

"Ren's favorite rule for catching a criminal is

only three words," Chase said slowly. "Follow the money."

"How does that apply to Harlan—or Lonnie, for that matter?" Raine asked, looking up at him.

"I doubt Harlan siphoned money from Marcus's holdings and deposited it in his Wolf Creek bank account. Which means he's probably hidden it somewhere." Chase covered her hand with his where it rested on his knee.

"Like in the vault at the ranch house," Zach said.

"Maybe," Chase agreed. "Or maybe he was smart enough to invest it somewhere and cover his tracks."

"But how would we find out where?" Trey asked, frustrated. "Doesn't that bring us back to breaking into the vault and hoping we find evidence?"

"Unless we can find another way…" Lori said.

She'd been silent up until now. Everyone turned to stare at her.

"Do you know of one?" Trey asked.

"I've always thought if you can't go over the top of a mountain, go around it, and if that won't work, dig a tunnel through it." She looked around the room. "I don't know Harlan, but from what I've heard about him from all of you, he sounds arrogant and self-important."

Raine rolled her eyes. "That's definitely Harlan—plus a lot of other unflattering adjectives."

A murmur of agreement went round the room.

"Arrogant people are more likely to hire someone to look after their books, not make entries themselves. Does Harlan have a bookkeeper on staff?" Lori asked. "Did he have one a couple of years ago when he took over managing the properties and businesses after Marcus became ill?"

Trey stared at her for a moment, and then a grin broke over his face and he grabbed her to drop a swift, hard kiss on her lips.

"Babe, you're brilliant." He looked at Chase. "And she's right, isn't she? Harlan must have a bookkeeper."

"As far as I know he uses the same one Marcus had for years—Anne Davis. She has an office here in town."

"I can't see Anne cooperating in a scheme to cheat Marcus," Zach said. "They were really tight—he was her first client when she started up straight out of college."

"I agree," Rachel put in. "I remember when Granddad hired her. It must have been twenty or more years ago. She used to come to the house for business meetings and stay for dinner—she adored

Granddad. I don't see her doing anything that would harm him."

"It sounds as if it might be a dead end, but I think we should explore it." Chase looked around the room. "Any other ideas?"

"Not from me," Trey answered, noting the others shaking their heads.

"Then I suggest Zach and I pay a visit to Anne."

"Just you and Zach?" Trey didn't appreciate being excluded.

"We can't all go. If Harlan notices us traveling in a pack he's going to guess we're up to something, and we want him to keep on feeling safe and unsuspecting. I'm going because I've interviewed potential witnesses before, and Zach's coming along to give the appearance of legitimate family concern. Of course," he added, "if she won't cooperate, we don't have any legal standing. We can't force her to answer questions."

"Yes, but if she stalls, we'll know we might be on the right track," Lori said.

"I suggest we meet back here tomorrow to go over what we've learned." Chase rose. "In the meantime, everybody keep brainstorming. As Lori said, there's a way to solve this. We just have to find it."

The following afternoon they all returned to Trey's apartment, but Chase and Zach didn't have good news.

"Anne Davis seems to be honest," Chase said.

"And she sure as hell doesn't like Harlan," Zach added. "Which isn't a surprise."

"She also told us she thought Harlan was up to no good before Marcus died, but she had no proof. She remained as bookkeeper when Marcus got sick and she questioned Harlan about the drop in the company's income. But he gave her vague responses and she didn't have any hard evidence to take to the sheriff."

"And he stopped using her agency a few months after Marcus died," Zach added.

"Who took over?" Trey asked.

"A firm in Helena. Ren's checking them out, but we have to be careful not to alert Harlan."

"Damn." Trey scrubbed his hands down his face. A headache was beginning to throb at his temple. "We're back to square one, aren't we?"

The room fell silent. Luke stared at the floor, his face gloomy.

The shrill ring of the telephone broke the quiet, making everyone jump.

"I'll get it." Luke reached behind him and

picked up the portable receiver from the counter-top. "Yeah?" A bemused smile curled his mouth. "Mom? What's up?"

His sister Jessie lifted her eyebrows and met Chase's questioning gaze. "Did you tell Mom we were going to be here?" she said softly.

He shook his head. "Not me."

"Okay, we're on our way. 'Bye." Luke set the receiver back in its base and stood. "We have to go out to the ranch."

"Is everything okay?" Jessie asked, sounding worried.

"I'm not sure." Luke swept the group. "Hannah Rimes is sitting in Mom's living room and says she won't leave until she talks to us. All of us, especially you, Trey."

"Who's Hannah Rimes?" Lori asked.

"She's the mother of Carl and Bobby Rimes, the brothers who hit Trey over the head and stole his SUV."

"What in heaven's name do you suppose she wants?" Lori asked.

"I don't know," Trey said grimly. "But I damn sure want to find out."

Mindful of not being conspicuous, they left in

pairs by different exits, several minutes apart and met up at John and Margaret's ranch.

Margaret rose as they entered, her eyes widening for a moment as she took in the four couples.

"Here you are," she said, recovering quickly, smiling and gesturing them forward. "Hannah, these are my children and their partners—Chase and Raine, Luke and Rachel and Jessie and Zach. And this is Trey Harper and Lori Ashworth."

Trey didn't remember Hannah Rimes and wasn't sure if he'd met her before. She was a tall, spare woman with gray hair, dressed in a tailored blue suit with navy low-heeled pumps. She sat stiffly erect in the upholstered chair, her spine at least three inches from the cushioned back, her hands folded in her lap. She didn't seem nervous, he thought, but her chin and expression held resolve. Her nod of response to Margaret's introductions was abrupt and determined.

"Please, sit down everyone," Margaret urged. "Hannah has something she wants to discuss with you."

Lori took a seat on the sofa next to Jessie but Trey didn't sit, choosing instead to stand behind her.

The older woman looked directly at Trey. "The sheriff tells me that my sons, Carl and Bobby, are accused of attacking you and stealing your car."

"That's my understanding," he said evenly, wondering where this was going.

"I'm not saying they didn't do it," she said, her gaze unwavering and focused. "And I'm not saying they did. I want to make that clear."

"Okay," he replied when it became obvious she waited for his confirmation.

"The sheriff tells me if my boys come home, they'll be arrested and tried for assault and probably kidnapping and if they're convicted, they'll do time." She glanced at Chase. He didn't respond, his face looked carved in granite. "Like any mother, I want my sons home. But I don't want them sent to prison."

"I'm not sure what I can do about that," Trey said when she paused to study him.

"You're the only one who can change things. At least, that's what the sheriff said." She looked from him to Chase once more, before returning to fix Trey with a level gaze. "I figure it's unlikely you'll help my boys, not after what they did to you. But I have information I think you might want and I'm willing to trade it for my sons' freedom."

Trey heard Lori stifle a quiet gasp. His eyes held Hannah's. "What is it?"

"Before I tell you, will you agree to talk to the

sheriff about not bringing charges against Carl and Bobby?"

"Not until I know what you've got," he responded. "All I can promise you is that if it's good enough, I'll see what I can do. If it isn't, then they're on their own."

Her mouth compressed in a thin line as she considered him. "Very well," she said crisply. "For several years, and up until this afternoon, I was Harlan Kerrigan's housekeeper." She ignored the collective hiss of indrawn breaths and continued.

"My boys went to work for Harlan not quite a year ago. At first I was grateful to him for taking them on. They'd been involved in a few scrapes with the law and if he hadn't hired them, they would have had to leave Wolf Creek to find work. Things went well for a while, but then I learned Harlan had my boys doing stuff besides ranching, things I didn't approve of.

"That's when I started eavesdropping on his telephone conversations whenever I could. I wanted ammunition to force him to assign my boys honest work. And that's how I found out about the woman who's been blackmailing him."

"He was being blackmailed?" Jessie asked, eyebrows winging upward. "How do you know?"

"I overheard him on the phone. It wasn't her he was talking to, it was her sister. The woman was sick and the sister wanted him to send money for the doctors' bills. But Harlan refused, saying he'd given her a fortune over the last fifteen years. Then a month later, the sister called back, and this time I managed to pick up the other phone. She told Harlan the woman had died and she was going to make him pay for not helping when she'd asked. They argued about it for several minutes before the woman got hysterical and said she'd turn the pictures over to the McClouds. Harlan laughed and told her that if she wanted to tangle with that family, go ahead. He said Chase was dangerous and she'd be sorry, not him. She screamed at him and said in that case she'd hand them over to the Harpers instead and hung up."

"This is all very interesting, but I'm not sure it's worth asking the sheriff to drop battery charges," Trey told her.

"This isn't what I want to trade—it's complicated and I needed to tell you what led up to my boys stealing—" she caught herself "—*allegedly* stealing your car."

Trey nodded, and she continued.

"Carl called me a few days ago and told me

Harlan thought the woman had sent you photographs and asked him and Bobby to watch you. When you left town one night, they followed. He didn't tell me what happened next, but I've heard that's the night you went missing."

"So far," Trey said evenly, anger swelling at the confirmation that Harlan was involved in his assault, "all you've given me are more reasons for your sons to go to jail."

"I know. I'm telling you this to make you understand that Harlan was behind the attack on you. Which leads me to the relevant point. I think you and you—" her eyes flicked to Chase "—might be more interested in seeing Harlan go to prison."

"We are." Chase's voice was remote, his face unreadable.

"Good." She nodded, one abrupt movement of her head. "Before I married the boys' father and moved to Wolf Creek, I worked as an assistant to an accountant in Havre. I kept books for Harlan while I was his housekeeper. He asked me to keep two sets while Marcus was alive, one for Kerrigan Holdings, and another that were his personal records. I'm not trained as a CPA, but it was clear to me there was something odd about the documents."

Trey and Lori exchanged glances. Her eyes were wide with growing comprehension. He suspected his own held triumph.

"Are you willing to testify in a court of law about what you know?" Jessie asked.

"Are you willing to help my boys stay out of jail, Mr. Harper?" Though her voice was crisp, Hannah's hands were clasped tightly together, her spare body stiff with apprehension.

"If we can prove Harlan coerced them," he said. "He'll deny it, of course, and I don't know if your word against his will convince a judge and jury, but it's worth a shot."

Hannah leaned forward and picked up her purse, tucked next to her feet. "It's not my word against his." She opened the bag and pulled out a thick file. "I made a copy of the records while I was working as Harlan's bookkeeper."

"Oh. My. God," Rachel breathed, her words loud in the stunned silence.

"Mrs. Rimes." Trey crossed the room and planted a kiss on the startled woman's cheek. "I'll talk to the sheriff and do what I can to make sure your sons come home. But you'd better tell them to stay out of my sight till this scar fades and my headaches are gone," he added.

"I will." Hannah's composure wavered, her eyes suddenly damp.

"Does Harlan know you have that file?" Chase asked her.

"I don't think so. I certainly didn't tell him. I'm concerned about going back to the house, though. I've asked him several times how he was planning to help Carl and Bobby but he was always evasive. I asked him again at lunch today, and he was irritable, told me there wasn't anything he could do and that the boys would have to stay in Belize until things calmed down in Wolf Creek." She looked at Margaret. "That's when I decided to come here. I left Harlan a message on his answering machine, telling him I was quitting. I didn't pack anything—I didn't want him to know I wasn't going back. I just tucked the file in my purse and drove down the highway like I was heading to town, just as I always do on my day off. I don't feel safe going back there, though. I hate to think what he might do if he finds out I talked to you."

"Good call," Trey said. "For sure you should keep away from Harlan. In fact, we'll work out protection and a safe place for you to lay low until he and Lonnie are both in custody."

"She can sleep here tonight," Margaret interrupted. "And if Harlan should be foolish enough to come and find you, my husband would be more than pleased to greet him with a shotgun."

"Chase and I will stay, too," Luke said. "Just in case Dad needs any help."

Hannah's posture eased. "Thank you," she said with obvious gratitude.

"In the meantime, I'll take the file." Trey held out his hand and she gave it to him without hesitation. "What made you decide to make a copy of the books?" he asked, curious.

"I knew there was something fishy about the receipts he gave me," she said. "And I didn't feel he was trustworthy. If there were allegations of misdeeds down the road, I wanted to be able to prove I wasn't involved."

"Smart move," Chase commented.

"I'll take Hannah upstairs to her room," Margaret said, "and leave you all to whatever comes next."

They murmured good-night as Margaret took the older woman's arm. When they disappeared through the doorway, Lori stood up and moved toward Trey.

"She's nothing like I imagined the mother of

two criminals to be," she commented. "In fact, she reminded me of my third grade schoolteacher, a very proper, law-abiding woman."

"I vaguely remember hearing gossip about Hannah and her husband," Rachel explained. "Evidently, he was as rough as she is refined. Unfortunately, the boys seem to take after their father instead of their mother."

"Can you really keep her sons from going to jail, Trey?" Lori asked.

"I'm not sure. Can I, Jessie?"

"As the victim of the assault, the court will take into account your recommendations." Jessie shrugged. "But it's really up to the judge."

"Then I hope, for Hannah's sake, that he cuts them some slack. Her sons might not deserve it, but Hannah does."

"I agree."

"Let's take a look at Hannah's file."

"Think we can make sense out of it?" Luke said.

"Between an attorney and three business owners, all of whom keep their own books, I hope the answer is yes," Trey said. "But if not, I bet Anne Davis will help us."

"I'll call her." Jessie picked up the phone. "Might as well have as much input as we can get."

* * *

Five days later, armed with a search warrant, the sheriff's department descended on Harlan Kerrigan's ranch headquarters. They drilled open the safe and took the contents—accounting records and a staggering amount of cash—into custody. At the same time, the police arrested Harlan at his estate in Helena and much to everyone's surprise, also nabbed Lonnie. He had ten thousand dollars in his wallet, together with a one-way ticket to Brazil.

The McCloud clan gathered at Raine and Trey's restaurant, pushing together several tables in the back to accommodate the group.

John brought champagne. "Margaret ordered this," he announced, handing the case to their waiter. "We'll need glasses for everyone, son, and keep opening bottles until they're all empty."

"Yes, sir."

Champagne flutes were passed around the table and John raised his. "Here's to a new era in Wolf Creek. Harlan's power is broken, he'll never again threaten our family or the peace of this town." He grinned and looked at Zach Kerrigan, his mother, Judith, and sister, Rachel. "And here's to the rest of the Kerrigans, who are living proof that they're not all bad. And who, thank God, ended the feud between our families in the best way possible—by marrying McClouds."

Luke whistled, a loud piercing sound that had Rachel wincing.

"And here's to justice," John continued. "It's been a long time coming."

"Hear, hear." Chase touched his flute to his father's and then tipped it up and drained it.

Raine leaned across and kissed his cheek.

"I think we should toast the newly engaged couple." Margaret beamed at Raine and Chase.

Chase planted his lips on his fiancée's. When he finally let her go, the table burst into cheers.

"Congratulations, you two." Trey smiled at his sister's flushed cheeks.

"Here's our food," Jessie said, stealing her husband's champagne when Zach turned away to answer a question from her brother Luke.

The rowdy group quieted only slightly as they ate. After dessert, they went next door to the saloon to continue the celebration, taking the remaining champagne with them.

Lori took turns dancing with the McClouds and Zach, and finally settled into Trey's arms. They moved slowly around the floor without speaking.

"I suppose I'll be going home tomorrow," she finally said, her face tucked against his throat.

He stiffened. "Why?"

"Now that Lonnie's in custody, Mom and I are safe in Granger. And I need to get back to work," she explained. "Ralph's probably tearing his hair out, trying to manage both the restaurant and the bar."

"Do you want to leave?"

She wasn't sure how to answer that. Did *he* want her to leave? He'd never said he loved her, never asked her to stay with him here in Wolf Creek. He'd told her he wanted to keep her out of danger, that he felt responsible for causing Lonnie's intrusion in their lives, but that wasn't the same as loving her. The sex was amazing, at least for her. But still, he'd never said the words she'd waited to hear.

"I think it's time," she said finally.

"The hell it is," he muttered.

He took her hand and led her off the floor, tugging her through a side door and up the back stairs to his apartment.

"Trey, what are you...?"

He didn't turn on the lights. Instead he backed her against the wall and kissed her. She went under in a heady rush. She couldn't think while his mouth was on hers, wicked and clever, making her blood heat and her bones melt.

When he lifted his head at last, she was breathless, barely able to focus.

"I don't want you to go back to Granger," he told her.

"I have to. Who'll run the business?"

"Let Ralph do it."

"He can't—he's a great chef but keeping books and managing employees drives him crazy. Besides, he and Mom would kill each other in less than a month."

"Then let Kari take over. She and Mason make a great team and they're both smart and ambitious. It's a win-win situation."

"Trey, why are you doing this? You know I can't stay here."

"Why not? Is it the apartment? I'll buy you a house. If I can't find one like your home in Granger, I'll build it for you. And you can duplicate the gardens—I know you love flowers."

She laughed, touched. "I do love flowers, Trey, and it's sweet of you to notice. But you can't buy me a house—I have to go back."

"Why?" His voice deepened, husky with restraint. "I know it's too soon for you to forgive me, Lori, but I meant what I said. I'll do whatever it takes to make it up to you for lying when I pretended to be Troy Jones. Tell me how to convince you."

"I believe at first you felt you had no choice— but after a while, I thought you should have trusted me and told me the truth."

"You're right." His voice was tinged with disgust. "I didn't tell you because I was a selfish bastard."

She felt her eyes widen with shock. "That's pretty harsh," she began.

"No," he interrupted. "It's not—I had other reasons, good reasons, for not telling you. But they don't matter, not in the long run. There's no excuse for my not being straight with you. It was wrong. I screwed up and I'm sorry."

She stared at him. "When I called and told you Lonnie had wrecked our house, you came immediately."

"Of course I did."

She thought about the other things he'd done for her, like fixing her dishwasher on his day off, helping Ralph in the kitchen without being paid, listening to Risa's chatter. Did she really not trust him? "That's not a selfish act."

"Thanks for the kind words, but I wanted you

and couldn't bear for you to stop seeing me. That was the real reason behind not admitting I wasn't the real Troy Jones."

"You wanted to keep seeing me?" she said faintly.

"Of course." He leaned into her, brushing soft kisses over her throat, the arch of her cheekbones and the corners of her mouth. "I knew you'd kick me to the curb if you discovered I was lying. You're not the kind of woman to put up with some guy blowing smoke—you're too smart. The truth is," he said starkly, "I didn't want to lose you. But it's happening anyway. You're going back to Granger." He rested his forehead against hers. "How the hell am I going to court you when you're all those miles away?" he whispered. "Am I going to have to move to Granger till I convince you to change your mind?"

"You'd move to Granger?" she said in disbelief.

"If I have to. I'd much rather you stayed here."

"I can't just move into your apartment and live with you," she said.

"So we'll fly to Vegas and get married tomorrow. We could be back in a few days."

Stunned, she stared at him. He clearly wasn't conscious of dropping a bombshell because he kept exploring her face with his lips, his hair brushing her cheek as he nipped the lobe of her ear, then licked it soothingly.

"Mmhh. Wait…" She caught his head in her hands and tugged him away from her. "I can't think when you're doing that."

He smiled, a sensual curve of his mouth that made her tremble.

"Stop it." She tried to sound stern and failed miserably. "What do you mean we could get married tomorrow?"

"I mean it's a short flight to Vegas. I thought you'd want a big wedding like the one Raine's planning, but if Vegas works for you, we can be there in a few hours."

"Are you asking me to marry you?" she said bluntly, exasperated.

"Of course I am. I did." He frowned at her. She glared back. "I asked you to stay in Wolf Creek— so I could court you, we could get engaged, then get married, have kids, grow old together and sit in rocking chairs," he said, carefully enunciating the words. "What part of that didn't you understand?"

"You never asked me to marry you."

"Yes, I did."

"No," she snapped, "you didn't."

"Well, I'm asking you now. Will you marry me?"

She opened her mouth to tell him that growling at her wasn't earning him points when she realized that beneath his scowl lurked a hint of vulnerable uncertainty.

"That depends."

"On what?"

"On whether or not you love me."

"Of course I love you." He pressed her against the wall again, pinning her with his weight, his hips trapping hers. "I walked into your bar and fell head over heels. I didn't think it could happen—thought that was just a fairy tale meant for little kids—but it was real." He tucked her hair behind her ear. "I'm crazy about you."

"I thought it was just the great sex," she whispered, her heart lurching at the look on his face.

"Oh, the sex is amazing," he agreed. "But so is everything else about you." He kissed her until they both had to stop to breathe. "Marry me," he ground out. "Say yes."

"Yes," she murmured.

"Thank God." He swung her into his arms and carried her into the bedroom.

* * * * *

*Set in darkness beyond the ordinary world.
Passionate tales of life and death.
With characters' lives ruled by laws the
everyday world can't begin to imagine.*

n●cturne

*It's time to discover the Raintree trilogy...
New York Times bestselling author
LINDA HOWARD
brings you the dramatic first book
RAINTREE: INFERNO*

**The Ansara Wizards are rising and the
Raintree clan must rejoin the battle against
their foes, testing their powers, relationships
and forcing upon them lives they never could
have imagined before...**

*Turn the page for a sneak preview
of the captivating first book
in the Raintree trilogy,
RAINTREE: INFERNO by LINDA HOWARD
On sale April 25.*

Dante Raintree stood with his arms crossed as he watched the woman on the monitor. The image was in black and white to better show details; color distracted the brain. He focused on her hands, watching every move she made, but what struck him most was how uncommonly *still* she was. She didn't fidget or play with her chips, or look around at the other players. She peeked once at her down card, then didn't touch it again, signaling for another hit by tapping a fingernail on the table. Just because she didn't seem to be paying attention to the other players, though, didn't mean she was as unaware as she seemed.

"What's her name?" Dante asked.

"Lorna Clay," replied his chief of security, Al Rayburn.

"At first I thought she was counting, but she doesn't pay enough attention."

"She's paying attention, all right," Dante murmured. "You just don't see her doing it." A card counter had to remember every card played. Supposedly counting cards was impossible with the number of decks used by the casinos, but there were those rare individuals who could calculate the odds even with multiple decks.

"I thought that, too," said Al. "But look at this piece of tape coming up. Someone she knows comes up to her and speaks, she looks around and starts chatting, completely misses the play of the people to her left—and doesn't look around even when the deal comes back to her, just taps that finger. And damn if she didn't win. Again."

Dante watched the tape, rewound it, watched it again. Then he watched it a third time. There had to be something he was missing, because he couldn't pick out a single giveaway.

"If she's cheating," Al said with something like respect, "she's the best I've ever seen."

"What does your gut say?"

Al scratched the side of his jaw, considering. Finally, he said, "If she isn't cheating, she's the luckiest person walking. She wins. Week in, week out, she wins. Never a huge amount, but I ran the numbers and she's into us for about five grand a week. Hell, boss, on her way out of the casino she'll stop by a slot machine, feed a dollar in and walk away with at least fifty. It's never the same machine, either. I've had her watched, I've had her followed, I've even looked for the same faces in the casino every time she's in here, and I can't find a common denominator."

"Is she here now?"

"She came in about half an hour ago. She's playing blackjack, as usual."

"Bring her to my office," Dante said, making a swift decision. "Don't make a scene."

"Got it," said Al, turning on his heel and leaving the security center.

Dante left, too, going up to his office. His face was calm. Normally he would leave it to Al to deal with a cheater, but he was curious. How was she doing it? There were a lot of bad cheaters, a few good ones, and every so often one would come along who was the stuff of which legends were made: the cheater who didn't get caught, even when people were alert and the camera was on him—or, in this case, her.

It was possible to simply be lucky, as most people understood luck. Chance could turn a habitual loser into a big-time winner. Casinos, in fact, thrived on that hope. But luck itself wasn't habitual, and he knew that what passed for luck was often something else: cheating. And there was the other kind of luck, the kind he himself possessed, but it depended not on chance but on who and what he was. He knew it was an innate power and not Dame Fortune's erratic smile. Since power like his was rare, the odds made it likely the woman he'd been watching was merely a very clever cheat.

Her skill could provide her with a very good living, he thought, doing some swift calculations in his head. Five grand a week equaled $260,000 a year, and that was just from his casino. She probably hit them all, careful to keep the numbers relatively low so she stayed under the radar.

He wondered how long she'd been taking him, how long she'd been winning a little here, a little there, before Al noticed.

The curtains were open on the wall-to-wall window in his office, giving the impression, when one first opened the door, of stepping out onto a covered balcony. The glazed window faced west, so he could catch the sunsets. The sun was low now, the sky painted in purple and gold. At his home in the mountains, most of the windows faced east, affording him views of the sunrise. Something in him needed both the greeting and the goodbye of the sun. He'd always been drawn to sunlight, maybe because fire was his element to call, to control.

He checked his internal time: four minutes until sundown. Without checking the sunrise tables every day, he knew exactly when the sun would slide behind the mountains. He didn't own an alarm clock. He didn't need one. He was so acutely attuned to the sun's position that he had only to check within himself to know the time. As for waking at a particular time, he was one of those people who could tell himself to wake at a certain time, and he did. That talent had nothing to do with being Raintree, so he didn't have to hide it; a lot of perfectly ordinary people had the same ability.

He had other talents and abilities, however, that

did require careful shielding. The long days of summer instilled in him an almost sexual high, when he could feel contained power buzzing just beneath his skin. He had to be doubly careful not to cause candles to leap into flame just by his presence, or to start wildfires with a glance in the dry-as-tinder brush. He loved Reno; he didn't want to burn it down. He just felt so damn *alive* with all the sunshine pouring down that he wanted to let the energy pour through him instead of holding it inside.

This must be how his brother Gideon felt while pulling lightning, all that hot power searing through his muscles, his veins. They had this in common, the connection with raw power. All the members of the far-flung Raintree clan had some power, some heightened ability, but only members of the royal family could channel and control the earth's natural energies.

Dante wasn't just of the royal family, he was the Dranir, the leader of the entire clan. "Dranir" was synonymous with king, but the position he held wasn't ceremonial, it was one of sheer power. He was the oldest son of the previous Dranir, but he would have been passed over for the position if he hadn't also inherited the power to hold it.

Behind him came Al's distinctive knock on the

door. The outer office was empty, Dante's secretary having gone home hours before. "Come in," he called, not turning from his view of the sunset.

The door opened, and Al said, "Mr. Raintree, this is Lorna Clay."

Dante turned and looked at the woman, all his senses on alert. The first thing he noticed was the vibrant color of her hair, a rich, dark red that encompassed a multitude of shades from copper to burgundy. The warm amber light danced along the iridescent strands, and he felt a hard tug of sheer lust in his gut. Looking at her hair was almost like looking at fire, and he had the same reaction.

The second thing he noticed was that she was spitting mad.

nocturne™

IT'S TIME TO DISCOVER
THE RAINTREE TRILOGY...

There have always been those among us
who are more than human...

Don't miss the dramatic first book by
New York Times bestselling author

LINDA
HOWARD

RAINTREE:
Inferno

On sale May.

Raintree: Haunted by Linda Winstead Jones
Available June.

Raintree: Sanctuary by Beverly Barton
Available July.

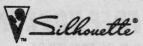

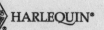

American ROMANCE®

A THREE-BOOK SERIES BY BELOVED AUTHOR

Judy Christenberry

Dallas Duets
What's behind the doors of
the Yellow Rose Lane apartments?
Love, Texas-style!

THE MARRYING KIND
May 2007

Jonathan Davis was many things—a millionaire,
a player, a catch. But he'd never be a husband.
For him, "marriage" equaled "mistake." Diane Black
was a forever kind of woman, a babies-and-minivan
kind of woman. But John was confident he could
date her and still avoid that trap.
Until he kissed her...

Also watch for:
DADDY NEXT DOOR
January 2007

MOMMY FOR A MINUTE
August 2007

Available wherever Harlequin books are sold.

www.eHarlequin.com

HARM07JC

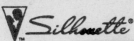

COMING NEXT MONTH